ADVANCED

lighthouse 2

Grammarmaster

Deinen Grammarmaster findest du auch in der **Cornelsen Lernen App**.

Siehst du eines dieser Symbole in deinem Grammarmaster, findest du in der App …

- alle **Erklärfilme**
- **Lösungen** zu den Aufgaben

Cornelsen

ADVANCED lighthouse 2

Grammarmaster

Im Auftrag des Verlages erarbeitet von
James Styring, Charlbury

In Zusammenarbeit mit der Englischredaktion
Klaus Unger (Projektleitung), Anja Zieschang

Beratende Mitwirkung
Daniel Henn, Frankfurt/Main; Christina Sieber, Schorndorf

Lizenzmanagement
Silke Kirchhoff

Illustrationen
Matthias Pflügner, Berlin
Irina Zinner, Hamburg

Fotos
Anja Poehlmann, Brighton
Für die freundliche Unterstützung danken wir der Varndean School, Brighton

Umschlaggestaltung
Rosendahl, Berlin

Layoutkonzept
Klein & Halm, Berlin

Layout und technische Umsetzung
PER MEDIEN & MARKETING GmbH, Braunschweig

Druck
AZ Druck und Datentechnik GmbH, Kempten

PEFC-zertifiziert
Dieses Produkt stammt aus nachhaltig bewirtschafteten Wäldern und kontrollierten Quellen
PEFC/04-31-2260
www.pefc.de

www.cornelsen.de

1. Auflage, 1. Druck 2024
978-3-06-034607-3

Hello again!
The last day of the holidays

Erklär-film

REVISION: Das present progressive

Mit dem *present progressive* sagst du, was jemand jetzt gerade tut. Du beschreibst damit auch, was auf Bildern passiert. Signalwörter für das *present progressive* sind: now (jetzt, gerade), at the moment (im Moment), today (heute).

Das *present progressive* besteht aus zwei Teilen:
be + *verb* + *-ing*
is *watching*

She's looking happy in the photo. (Sie sieht glücklich aus auf dem Foto.)

My parents aren't making lunch today. (Meine Eltern machen heute kein Mittagessen.)

What are you doing at the moment? (Was machst du gerade?)

be
I am / 'm not
he/she/it is / isn't
we/you/they are / aren't

► SB p. 11, p. 200

1 REVISION A day on the beach

What are or aren't the people doing at the moment? Look at the picture and write positive and negative sentences. *Was machen die Leute gerade? Was machen sie nicht? Schreibe bejahte und verneinte Sätze.*

1 Sonya *is playing* (play) volleyball. She *isn't swimming* (swim).

2 Josh ____________ (stand) on the beach. He ____________ (surf).

3 Ben and his dad ____________ (build) a sandcastle. They ____________ (have) a picnic.

4 Justine and her friend ____________ (take) a photo. They ____________ (sleep).

5 Holly's dog ____________ (eat). It ____________ (run) for a ball.

► Check

Unit 1
Travel and holidays

Erklär-film

Das simple past mit *be*

Mit dem *simple past* sprichst du über Dinge, die in der Vergangenheit geschehen sind. Du verwendest es oft mit Zeitangaben wie yesterday (gestern), last week (letzte Woche), in 2022 (2022), ago (vor).

Das Verb *be* hat besondere *simple past*-Formen:

A **bejahte und verneinte Aussagesätze**

I / He / She / It / Noah / Mum	was / wasn't	at home.
You / We / They / My friends	were / weren't	at home.

B **Fragen**

	Was	he / she	at home?
	Were	you / they	at home?
Where	were	you	?

▸ SB p. 13, pp. 200–201

1 How was your holiday?

Circle the right words. *Kreise die richtigen Wörter ein.*

Toby How was / were your holiday?

Lucy It was / were great, thanks. We was / were in Spain. Was / Were you here in Brighton all the time?

Toby No, we wasn't / weren't. We was / were in Wales for two weeks. It was / were wet and windy. Was / Were the weather good in Spain?

Lucy It was / were sunny every day. The weather was / were lovely!

2 The first day back at school

Look at the picture and complete the sentences with *was, were, wasn't* or *weren't*. *Schau dir das Bild an und vervollständige die Sätze mit* was, were, wasn't *oder* weren't.

1 Was ________ Noah's shirt blue? – No, it ________.

It ________ white.

2 ________ Sunita's skirt black? – Yes, it ________.

3 ________ Noah and Zane's uniforms the same? – Yes, they ________.

▸ Check

Erklär-film

Das simple past: Bejahte Aussagesätze mit regelmäßigen Verben

Bei regelmäßigen Verben hängst du *-ed* an das Verb an. Es gibt nur eine Form für alle Personen:

I/you/he/she/it/we/you/they talked, looked, watched, ...

! Beachte:

- Endet das Verb auf *-e*, hängst du nur *-d* an: *smile → smiled, like → liked, save → saved*
- Bei manchen Verben wird er Konsonant am Ende verdoppelt: *plan → planned, stop → stopped, travel → travelled*
- Ein *-y* nach Konsonant wird zu *-ied*: *cry → cried, worry → worried, tidy → tidied*

► SB p. 14, p. 201

3 Lisa's holiday

Lisa is talking about her last holidays. Complete her sentences. Use the verbs in the simple past.

Lisa erzählt von ihren letzten Ferien. Vervollständige ihre Sätze. Verwende die Verben im simple past.

My parents were at work, so I (1) stayed (stay) in Brighton in the holidays. Sunita was in Prague and Alice was in Wales, so it was quiet without my friends. I (2) ______ (visit) my grandma for some days. She's lovely – she lives in Hove. It's always fun at the beach, so I often (3) ______ (cycle) there in the holidays. I (4) ______ (play) beach volleyball and I (5) ______ (practise) stand up paddling. Sometimes I (6) ______ (watch) a film at the cinema at the Marina.

One night I was at Ravi's birthday party. We (7) ______ (talk), (8) ______ (listen) to music and (9) ______ (dance). Poor Ravi! He (10) ______ (worry) about his neighbours.

One weekend my dad and I (11) ______ (travel) to London. We (12) ______ (try) to visit all the sights, but there were too many. Dad and I (13) ______ (love) the city! I (14) ______ (like) the Pride Parade too. There were 300,000 people in Brighton that day.

► Check

Das simple past: Bejahte Aussagesätze mit unregelmäßigen Verben

Einige Verben haben unregelmäßige Formen im *simple past*, z. B.:

do	→	did	forget	→	forgot
have	→	had	hear	→	heard
run	→	ran	read	→	read

Diese Formen musst du lernen.

► SB p. 14, p. 201, pp. 312–313

4 Irregular verbs

a) **Complete the table. You can use the irregular verbs pages in your Student's book for help (pages 312–313).** *Vervollständige die Tabelle. Wenn du Hilfe brauchst, kannst du die unregelmäßigen Verben in deinem Schulbuch nachschlagen (Seiten 312–313).*

1 be	was / ______	7 ride	______
2 buy	______	8 sit	______
3 drink	______	9 sing	______
4 eat	______	10 swim	______
5 go	______	11 take	______
6 meet	______	12 wear	______

b) **Complete the sentences. Use simple past forms from the grammar box and from a.**
Vervollständige die Sätze. Verwende simple past-Formen aus dem Grammatikkasten sowie aus a.

1 We *were* at the Pride Parade two weeks ago.

2 I ______ a cool song on the radio yesterday.

3 She ______ her homework in the school library last Friday.

4 He ______ some messages on his phone an hour ago.

5 I ______ my new bike to school this morning.

6 We ______ a present for you in the toy shop last week.

7 My dad ______ a marathon in May.

8 Katie ______ at the table next to me yesterday.

9 Oh, no! I ______ about your birthday party.

10 We ______ juice in the break.

11 Marcus and I ______ at 11.30 last Sunday.

► Check

5 Lily and Alice's holidays

Complete the sentences with the simple past form of the verbs in the boxes.
Vervollständige die Sätze mit der simple past-Form der Verben in den Kästen.

borrow • do • ~~fly~~ • have • meet • ride • stay

Lily and her mum (1) flew ____________ to Poland and (2) ____________ at her aunt and uncle's house. They (3) ____________ lots of different things. One day they (4) ____________ her aunt and uncle's bikes and (5) ____________ around Krakow. Lily also (6) ____________ the children next door to aunt Svetlana's and they (7) ____________ lots of fun in the park.

be (2x) • cook • drink • go • love • sing • take

Alice (8) ____________ to Wales with her dad and her brother. It was a long journey – it (9) ____________ eight hours! They (10) ____________ on a campsite. It (11) ____________ a bit cold, but they (12) ____________ it! In the evenings they (13) ____________ barbecues. Then they (14) ____________ hot chocolate and they (15) ____________ songs by the fire.

6 What about you?

Write sentences about you. Use the simple past form of the verbs in brackets. Say when it happened.
Schreibe Sätze über dich. Verwende die simple past-Form der Verben in Klammern. Sag, wann es geschehen ist.

1 (talk) I talked to my grandma this morning.

2 (drink) ____________________

3 (play) ____________________

4 (eat) ____________________

► Check

Erklär-
film

Das simple past: Verneinte Aussagesätze

Willst du sagen, dass etwas nicht geschah, stellst du didn't vor den Infinitiv des Verbs. *Didn't* verwendest du bei allen Personen.

Ben didn't like the food. (Ben mochte das Essen nicht.)

We didn't go out last Friday. (Wir sind letzten Freitag nicht ausgegangen.)

► SB p. 20, p. 201

7 Scout's summer (1)

Complete the sentences. Use the simple past negative of the blue verbs.
Vervollständige die Sätze. Verwende die verneinte simple past-Form der blauen Verben.

1

Scout ate fish and chips.

She didn't eat ____________ burgers.

2

Scout flew over Brighton Pier.

She ____________ over Blackpool Pier.

3

Scout danced in the rain.

She ____________ in the sun.

4

Scout wore a tie.

She ____________ a blazer.

5

Scout walked on the pier.

She ____________ in the road.

6

Scout saw a lot of tourists.

She ____________ Lily or Zane.

► Check

8 Mistake or not?

Correct the mistakes. If there aren't any mistakes, put a tick (✓). *Korrigiere die Fehler. Wenn es keine Fehler gibt, dann mache ein Häkchen (✓).*

1 We don't go to the football match last week. Was it good? We didn't go

2 You didn't go to the cinema yesterday. ______

3 They went to London in the holidays. ______

4 Your teacher didn't gave you homework last week. ______

5 I didn't know about the party on Saturday night. Who was there? ______

6 It didn't rains last weekend. ______

9 Your last holidays

Write six positive or negative sentences about your last holidays. You can use the ideas in the pictures or your own ideas. *Schreibe sechs bejahte oder verneinte Sätze über deine letzten Ferien. Nutze dazu die Ideen in den Bildern oder deine eigenen Ideen.*

1

fly

2

buy

3

play

4
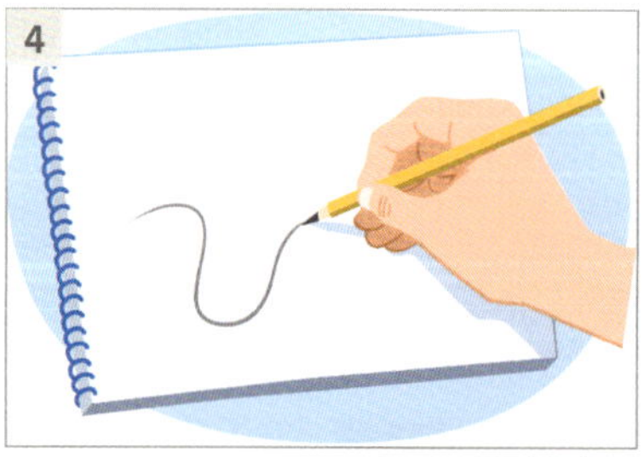
draw

5

cook

6

swim

______

______

______

______

______

▸ Check

10 Revision Scout's summer (2)

Complete the sentences about Scout with the simple past positive form of the verbs in the box.
Vervollständige die Sätze über Scout mit der bejahten simple past-Form der Verben im Kasten.

be • eat • enjoy • fly • give • relax

Scout wasn't away in the holidays. She (1) *was* ______ in Brighton all summer. She (2) ______ around the city and she (3) ______ the good weather. Scout (4) ______ on the beach and she (5) ______ a lot of food too. There (6) ______ lots of tourists and some of them (7) ______ their fish and chips to Scout!

11 Revision Reasons why

Write sentences in the simple past. *Schreibe Sätze im simple past.*

1 we / not go / to the cinema last weekend because we / not have / time
We didn't go to the cinema last weekend because we didn't have time.

2 Ravi / not visit / us last week because he / not get / our invitation
______

3 I / not finish / my pizza for lunch because I / not be / hungry
______

4 the students / not be / in class yesterday because it / not be / a school day
______

5 my sisters / not travel / to Brighton yesterday because they / not feel / well
______

6 I / not see / the Loch Ness Monster in Scotland because I / not go / to Loch Ness.
______

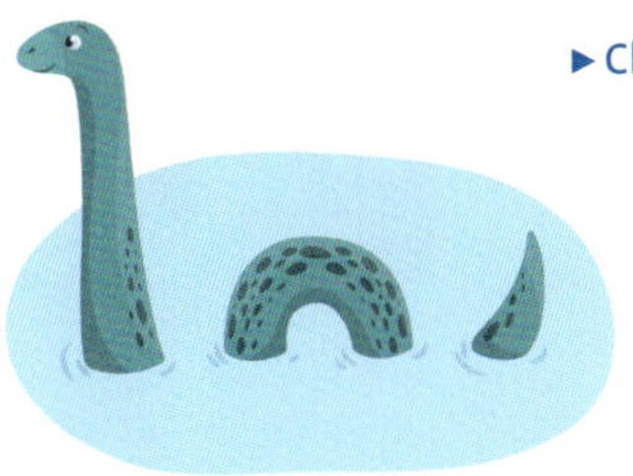

► Check

Unit 2
Friends and heroes

Erklär-film

Das simple past: Fragen und Kurzantworten

Fragen im *simple past* bildest du mit did und dem Infinitiv des Verbs. Auf Entscheidungsfragen antwortest du mit Kurzantworten.

Did Gina visit her friends last week? – Yes, she did. / No, she didn't.
(Hat Gina letzte Woche ihre Freunde besucht? – Ja, hat sie. / Nein, hat sie nicht.)

► SB p. 52, p. 202

1 Yes, I did!

a) **Write the questions.** *Schreibe die Fragen.*

1 Did ______ she play ______ football? (play) Yes, she did. ______

2 ______ they ______ to school? (walk) ______

3 ______ he ______ the homework? (do) ______

4 ______ we ______ shopping? (go) ______

5 ______ you ______ the train? (get) ______

6 ______ she ______ in the pool? (swim) ______

b) **Look at the pictures from last week. Write short answers.**
Sieh dir die Bilder von letzter Woche an. Schreibe Kurzantworten.

1

2

3

4

5

6

► Check

2 The friends' holidays

a) **Write questions. Put the words in the right order.** *Schreibe Fragen. Setze die Wörter in die richtige Reihenfolge.*

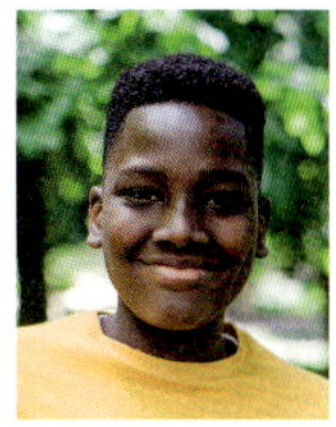

1 Sunita's family / did / visit / Prague?

Did Sunita's family visit Prague?

2 they / did / on a campsite? / stay ______

3 Noah / did / on holiday to Wales? / go ______

4 stay / in Brighton? / did / he ______

5 did / travel / to Poland? / Lily ______

6 she / her grandparents' house? / did / visit ______

7 to France? / did / go / Zane's family ______

8 their apartment / did / a pool? / have ______

b) **Match the short answers with the questions from a.** *Ordne die Kurzantworten den Fragen aus a zu.*

1 Yes, they did.	___ Yes, they did.	___ No, he didn't.	___ Yes, she did.
___ No, they didn't.	___ Yes, it did.	___ Yes, he did.	___ No, she didn't.

c) **Look at pages 12–13 in your Student's book and check your answers.** *Schau dir die Seiten 12–13 in deinem Schulbuch an und überprüfe die Antworten.*

3 Did you ...?

Write simple past questions. Answer the questions for you.
Schreibe Fragen im simple past. Beantworte die Fragen für dich.

1 you / do / sport last weekend?

Did you do sport last weekend? – Yes, I did.

2 you and your family / watch / TV last night?

______

3 you / meet / your friends at the weekend?

______

4 you / help / your parents this morning?

______

▸ Check

Erklär-film

Das simple past: Fragen mit Fragewort

Auch Fragen mit Fragewörtern bildest du mit *did*. Das Fragewort steht immer am Satzanfang.

Fragewort	did	Person	Verb im Infinitiv		
Where	*did*	*Lily*	*take*	*the photo?*	*(Wo hat Lily das Foto gemacht?)*
When	*did*	*she*	*take*	*the photo?*	*(Wann hat sie das Foto gemacht?)*

Wenn du nach dem Subjekt fragst (Wer oder was …?), dann bildest du die Frage ohne *did*.

Who helped Noah? (Wer half Noah?)

► SB p. 53, p. 202

4 Where did you meet your friends?

Write questions. Put the words in the right order.
Schreibe Fragen. Setze die Wörter in die richtige Reihenfolge.

who? – wer?
what? – was?
when? – wann?
where? – wo?
why? – warum?
how? – wie?

1 meet / your friends? / did / where / you ______

______

2 phone / Sunita / did / last night? / who ______

3 did / what / have / in his lunch box? / he ______

4 Emma / write / why / did / a poem? ______

5 finish / your homework? / did / you / when ______

5 Isla's holiday

Read Isla's answers. Then complete Livia's questions. Use the verbs in blue and a question word from the box. *Lies Islas Antworten. Vervollständige dann Livias Fragen. Verwende die Verben in Blau und ein Fragewort aus dem Kasten.*

how long • what • when • ~~where~~ • who

Livia (1) Where did ______ you go ______ on holiday?
Isla We went to Lake Garda in Italy.
Livia Nice! (2) ______ you ______ there?
Isla We stayed there for ten days.
Livia (3) ______ you ______ with?
Isla I went with my dad, my sister and my cousin.
Livia (4) ______ you ______ there?
Isla We did lots of things! We rode our bikes, we went swimming – and we ate pizzas!
Livia That sounds amazing. (5) ______ you ______ home?
Isla We got home in the last week of the holidays.

► Check

Indirekte Rede

Die indirekte Rede (*indirect speech*) verwendest du, wenn du berichtest, was jemand anderes sagt, schreibt oder denkt. Sätze in der indirekten Rede werden oft eingeleitet mit Verben wie *answer, say, tell sb., think*.

Melissa says (that) she likes her new school. (Melissa sagt, dass sie ihre neue Schule mag.)
The sign says (that) you can't sit here. (Auf dem Schild steht, dass man hier nicht sitzen darf.)

Personalpronomen, Pronomen und Verb musst du anpassen:

Peter says "I want to go to the library with my sister."
→ *Peter says (that) he wants to go to the library with his sister.*

► SB p. 51, p. 202

6 What they say

Read what they say. Then write their speech as indirect speech.
Lies, was sie sagen. Schreibe dann ihre Sätze in der indirekten Rede.

That („dass") kannst du weglassen.
Martin says that you're the best. =
Martin says you're the best.

Felix	Safira	Leon	Isa	Lev	Abena

Felix says that he can do some cool dance moves.

____

____

____

____

____

____

► Check

Nebensätze mit Konjunktionen

Konjunktionen verwendest du, um Sätze miteinander zu verknüpfen. Die Wortstellung im Hauptsatz und im Nebensatz ist immer gleich: subject – verb – object.

subject	verb	object	Konjunktion	subject	verb	object
I	*have*	*a snack*	*when*	*I*	*'m*	*hungry.*
They	*got*	*the bus*	*because*	*they*	*didn't want*	*to walk.*
Simon	*practises*	*the guitar*	*so*	*he*	*can join*	*a band.*

▸ SB p. 57, p. 203

7 Milo missed the bus

Read the conversation. Circle the right words. *Lies die Unterhaltung. Kreise die richtigen Wörter ein.*

because – weil
so – also, daher
when – als

Farah Hi, Milo! What's up?

Milo I'm annoyed because / so I missed the bus.

Farah Oh, no. What happened?

Milo I was a bit late, when / so I ran to High Street. Because / When I got to High Street, I heard the bus and I started to run really fast. I waved at the bus driver, but she didn't see me, when / so she closed the doors. The bus drove away because / when I arrived at the bus stop. It's so annoying!

8 Because I can't

Complete the sentences. *Vervollständige die Sätze.*

1 We can't go to the cinema because *we don't have any money*.
don't have / we / any money

2 I have lots of homework, so ______.
I / can't talk / for long

3 Dinner will be ready when ______.
you / home / get

4 I watch films in English because ______.
want to become / better in English / I

5 I downloaded his new album, so ______.
in the car / can play / you / it

▸ Check

9 Revision Quiz

a) **Complete the questions with the words from the box.**
Vervollständige die Fragen mit den Wörtern aus dem Kasten.

did (2x) • made • when • which • win • write • won

1 Where did ________ the 2024 Olympic Games take place?

2 Which famous book did Lewis Caroll ________?

3 Which country ________ the last Eurovision Song Contest?

4 ________ did Germany last ________ the FIFA World Cup?

5 ________ well-known song ________ DJ Robin & Schürze make in 2022?

6 Who ________ the Avatar films?

b) **Can you answer the questions? You can check your answers online.**
Kannst du die Fragen beantworten? Du kannst deine Lösungen im Internet überprüfen.

1 ________

2 ________

3 ________

4 ________

5 ________

6 ________

10 Revision Find the mistakes

Read the questions and answers. There's one mistake in each pair of sentences. Find the mistake and write the correct sentence. *Lies die Fragen und Antworten. In jedes Satzpaar hat sich ein Fehler eingeschlichen. Finde den Fehler und schreibe den korrekten Satz.*

Achte auf das *simple past* und die Konjunktionen in diesen Sätzen.

1 Where you went on holiday? – We went to Belek in Turkey.

Where did you go on holiday?

2 How did you get to school this morning? – I walked so it was a nice day.

____

3 You started school late yesterday? – Yes, we did. We started school at 10 a.m.

____

4 What you did buy at the shops? – I bought some clothes.

____

5 Did you see the cat because you got home last night? – No, I didn't.

____

► Check

Unit 3
Activities and games

Erklärfilm

Das Futur mit going to: Bejahte und verneinte Aussagen

Das Futur mit *going to* besteht immer aus drei Teilen:

am / is / are am not / isn't / aren't	+ going to	+ Infinitiv des Verbs

Mit *going to* sagst du, dass du etwas in der Zukunft plانst (*after school, tomorrow, next week*).
I'm going to bedeutetet „Ich werde" oder „Ich habe vor".

I'm going to go to a holiday camp this summer. (Ich werde diesen Sommer in ein Ferienlager fahren.)
My parents are going to buy a new car next month. (Meine Eltern haben vor, nächsten Monat ein neues Auto zu kaufen.)
Holly isn't going to visit her grandma tomorrow. (Holly wird morgen ihre Großmutter nicht besuchen.)

► SB p. 82, p. 203

1 Alma's blog

Read Alma's blog. Circle the correct words. *Lies Almas Blog. Kreise die richtigen Wörter ein.*

www.almasblog.example.com

We 're going to have / 'm going to have an activity week at our school. There are going to be / is going to be 30 activities and we can choose two. I love sport, so I 'm going to choose / 're going to choose football. Karate sounds good too, but I 'm not going to do / isn't going to do two sports activities. I'd like to try something creative, so I 're going to try / 'm going to try a screen printing workshop. My friends aren't going to do / isn't going to do the same as me. Anita are going to do / is going to do chess club and photography. Felix am going to study / is going to study local history and photography. Activity week is going to be / are going to be fun!

screen printing

2 Activity week plans

Complete the plans. Use *am/'m, is/'s, are/'re*. *Vervollständige die Pläne. Verwende* am/'m, is/'s, are/'re.

1 They ________ going to study local history.
2 I ________ not going to learn karate.
3 She ________ not going to do art.
4 Anita ________ going to try photography.
5 Some activities ________ going to be outdoors.
6 We ________ going to work with animals.

► Check

3 You're going to enjoy this!

Complete the sentences. Use positive (+) or negative (–) forms of the going to-future.
Vervollständige die Sätze. Verwende bejahte (+) und verneinte (–) Formen des going to-future.

1 You *'re going to enjoy* ______ the zip wire! (enjoy +)

2 I ______ to a pantomime. (go –)

3 She ______ to cook Thai food. (learn +)

4 This ______ an insect hotel. (be +)

5 We ______ with animals. (work –)

6 The show ______ at 7.30. (start +)

7 They ______ football after school. (practise –)

8 Thomas ______ us at the cinema. (meet +)

4 Jumbled words

Write sentences about the people's plans. *Schreibe Sätze über die Pläne der Leute.*

1 aren't / be / there / teachers / going to

______

2 going to / 're / toy animals / knit / we

______

3 plan / isn't / going to / a summer tea party / he

______

4 take / the school goats for walks / we / 're / going to

______

5 role-playing games / isn't / she / going to / try

______

5 What are you going to do?

Write four sentences about your plans. Write positive or negative sentences in the going to-future.
Schreibe vier Sätze über deine Pläne. Schreibe bejahte und verneinte Sätze im going to-future.

______

______

► Check

Erklär-film

Das Futur mit going to: Fragen und Kurzantworten

Bei Fragen stehen am, are oder is am Beginn des Fragesatzes, vor dem Subjekt.

Am I going to join the karate club? – Yes, I am. / No, I'm not. (Werde ich in den Karateclub eintreten?)
Is Peter going to meet Leo? – Yes, he is. / No, he isn't. (Hat Peter vor, Leo zu treffen?)
Are they going to make a cake for your party? – Yes, they are. / No, they aren't. (Haben sie vor, einen Kuchen für deine Party zu backen?)

▶ SB p. 83, p. 204

6 Questions and answers

Match the questions and short answers. *Ordne die Fragen und Kurzantworten zu.*

1 Are you going to learn the guitar?	A No, they aren't.
2 Is Emma going to make lunch?	B Yes, I am.
3 Am I going to pass the test?	C Yes, he is.
4 Are the teachers going to help us?	D No, she isn't.
5 Is Ben going to work?	E Yes, you are.

7 The friends' activity week plans

a) **What are the friends going to do? Write questions.** *Was werden die Freunde tun? Schreibe Fragen.*

1 Zane / about photography? / learn

Is Zane going to learn about photography? – *No*, he *isn't*.

2 Lily and Sunita / sports activities? / do

__________ – ______, they ______.

3 study / Noah / 'History in Brighton'?

__________ – ______, he ______.

4 'Tea party and show'? / Zane / choose

__________ – ______, he ______.

5 creative activities? / do / Lily and Noah

__________ – ______, they ______.

b) **Can you remember the four friends' plans? Complete the short answers.** *Kannst du dich an die Pläne der vier Freunde erinnern? Vervollständige die Kurzantworten.*

c) **Look at page 81 in your Student's book to check your answers.** *Schau dir Seite 81 in deinem Schulbuch an und überprüfe deine Antworten.*

▶ Check

Das Futur mit going to: Fragen mit Fragewort

Das Fragewort steht auch bei *going to* am Satzanfang.

What am I going to do? (Was werde ich tun?)
Who are you going to meet? (Wen wirst du treffen?)
Why is Zane going to talk to Ms Bond? (Warum wird Zane mit Frau Bond sprechen?)
Where are your teachers going to go? (Wo werden deine Lehrer hingehen?)

▸ SB p. 83, p. 204

8 Missing question words

Complete the questions with the question words. *Vervollständige die Fragen mit den Fragewörtern.*

how • what • when • where

1 ________________ is your family going to go on holiday?

2 ________________ are you going to do after school today?

3 ________________ is Simon going to play, now or later?

4 ________________ are we going to get to the airport?

9 Interview questions

a) **What are Alma's plans for activity week? Write interview questions in the going to-future.**
Was sind Almas Pläne für die Veranstaltungswoche? Schreibe Fragen im going to-future.

1 which / activity / you / choose? ________________

2 who / plan / the activity? ________________

3 where / you / do / the activity? ________________

4 when / it / start? ________________

5 how much / it / cost? ________________

6 why / you / enjoy / it? ________________

b) **Match the questions from a with the answers and write the right number 1–6 with the answer.**
Ordne die Fragen aus a und die Antworten zu und schreibe die richtige Zahl 1–6 neben die Antwort.

☐ A *In the park.*

☐ B *Footie Fans.*

☐ C *Because I love football!*

☐ D *Our PE teacher.*

☐ E *Next week.*

☐ F *It isn't going to cost anything.*

▸ Check

Erklär-film

Die Steigerung von Adjektiven: Komparativ

Mit den Steigerungsformen der Adjektive kannst du Dinge oder Personen miteinander vergleichen.

A Bei einsilbigen Adjektiven und zweisilbigen Adjektiven, die auf *-y* enden, hängst du *-er* an. Beachte die Schreibweise:

old	*older (than)*	*My mum is older than my dad.*
easy	*easier (than)*	*I think English is easier than French.*
big	*bigger (than)*	*Emre's dog is bigger than Nila's dog.*

B Hat das Adjektiv drei oder mehr Silben oder zwei Silben und endet nicht auf *-y*, steigerst du es mit more.

famous	*more famous (than)*	*Spiderman is more famous than Captain Planet.*
expensive	*more expensive (than)*	*A car is more expensive than a bike.*
interesting	*more interesting (than)*	*This book is more interesting than the others.*

▸ SB p. 85, p. 205

10 Superhero quiz

a) **Read the sentences and find out the superheroes' names. Write them under the pictures.**
Lies die Sätze und finde die Namen der Superhelden heraus. Schreibe sie unter die Bilder.

1 
2 
3 
4 
5 
6 

1 Lady Fight 2 ________ 3 ________ 4 ________ 5 ________ 6 ________

________ ________ ________ ________ ________ ________

1 Doctor Heart's cape is shorter than all the other capes.
2 Coolboy's hair is darker than Lady Fight's hair.
3 Captain Right is smaller than all the others.
4 Megastorm's hair is lighter than Captain Right's hair.
5 Mr Strong's mask is bigger than Captain Right and Megastorm's masks.

b) **What do you think? Complete the sentences.**
Was meinst du? Vervollständige die Sätze.

1 Doctor Heart is nicer ________ than Lady Fight ________. (nice)
2 Captain Right is ________ than ________. (interesting)
3 Megastorm is ________ than ________. (dangerous)
4 Coolboy is ________ than ________. (big)
5 Mr Strong is ________ than ________. (strong)
6 Lady Fight is ________ than ________. (scary)

Endet ein einsilbiges Adjektiv auf einen Vokal + Konsonant, verdoppelt sich der Konsonant. Ein stummes *-e* fällt weg.

big – bigger
nice – nicer

▸ Check

11 Three superheroes' cars

Compare the superheroes' cars. Complete the sentences with the comparative forms of the adjectives.
Vergleiche die Autos der Superhelden. Vervollständige die Sätze mit den Komparativen der Adjektive.

A

B

C

1 Car B is *newer than* ______ car A.
2 Car A is ______ car B.
3 Car C is ______ car A.
4 Car A is ______ car C.
5 Car B is ______ car C.
6 Car C is ______ car B.
7 Car C is ______ car A.

new
beautiful
fast
old
small
expensive
exciting

12 What's missing?

One word is missing in each sentence. Use the words from the box and write correct sentences.
Ein Wort fehlt in jedem Satz. Verwende die Wörter aus dem Kasten und schreibe korrekte Sätze.

as (2x) • aren't • is • than

Möchtest du sagen, dass etwas (nicht) genau gleich ist, verwendest du:

(not) as … as
as cool as (so cool wie)
not as expensive as (nicht so teuer wie)

1 Brighton is warm as London in summer.
Brighton is as warm as London in summer.

2 My sister as old as my best friend.
______

3 My brother is taller than you. You as tall as him.
______

4 Cars are quicker bikes.
______

5 My insect hotel isn't as cool the one you made.
______

▸ Check

Erklärfilm

Die Steigerung von Adjektiven: Superlativ

Möchtest du sagen, dass etwas am besten, größten, teuersten usw. ist, verwendest du den Superlativ.

A Bei einsilbigen Adjektiven und zweisilbigen Adjektiven, die auf *-y* enden, hängst du *-est* an.
Beachte wieder die Schreibweise:

old	*the oldest*	*Dima is the oldest boy in class.*
funny	*the funniest*	*Megastorm is the funniest superhero.*
big	*the biggest*	*We live in the biggest house in the road.*

B Hat das Adjektiv drei oder mehr Silben oder zwei Silben und endet nicht auf *-y*,
bildest du den Superlativ mit most.

beautiful	*the most beautiful*	*Roses are the most beautiful flowers.*
important	*the most important*	*This is the most important competition of the year.*

► SB p. 86, p. 205

13 Holiday places

a) **Write the superlative.** *Schreibe den Superlativ.*

	comparative	superlative
1 expensive	more expensive	the most expensive
2 rainy	rainier	the
3 warm	warmer	
4 cold	colder	
5 popular	more popular	

b) **Look at the information and complete the sentences with the correct superlative from a.**
Schau dir die Informationen an und vervollständige dann die Sätze mit den Superlativen aus a.

town	Brighton (England)	Inverness (Scotland)	Cork (Ireland)
popularity	❤️❤️❤️❤️❤️	❤️❤️❤️	❤️❤️❤️
price	💰💰	💰	💰💰💰
summer	☀️☀️☀️☀️☀️	☀️☀️☀️	☀️☀️☀️☀️
winter	🌨️🌨️	🌨️🌨️🌨️	🌨️
rain	🌧️🌧️🌧️	🌧️🌧️	🌧️🌧️🌧️🌧️🌧️

1 Cork and Inverness are popular holiday places, but Brighton is the most popular town.

2 Inverness isn't an expensive town. Brighton is more expensive and Cork is ____________ town.

3 Inverness and Cork are warm in summer, but Brighton is ____________ town.

4 Cork isn't very cold in winter. Brighton is colder and Inverness is ____________ town.

5 Inverness isn't very rainy. Brighton is rainier and Cork is ____________ town.

► Check

14 This is the best!

Complete the sentences with the superlatives of the adjectives in brackets. *Vervollständige die Sätze mit den Superlativen der Adjektive in Klammern.*

Diese unregelmäßigen Steigerungsformen musst du lernen:
good – better – the best
bad – worse – the worst

1 Tom is the happiest ______ person in our family. (happy)

2 This is ______ day of my life! (bad)

3 It's going to be ______ day of the year. (hot)

4 Scout is ______ seagull on the beach! (noisy)

5 Dungeons & Dragons is ______ role-playing game. (exciting)

6 Is this ______ activity this week? (good)

7 I think knitting is ______ course in activity week. (creative)

8 You took some great photos. This one is ______. (beautiful)

15 Zane and his family

Zane is talking about his family. Read the text and complete it with the superlative forms of the adjectives in the box. *Zane spricht über seine Familie. Lies den Text und vervollständige ihn mit den Superlativen der Adjektive im Kasten.*

active • long • noisy • old • tall • wonderful • young

I'm 12, but I'm not (1) ______ person in my family: my sister Holly is younger. She's seven.

Dad is 43. He's a bit older than Mum. He's (2) ______ person in the Adebayo family. Mum is 41.

I'm tall, but I'm not (3) ______ person in my family – yet! At the moment Dad is 3 cm taller than me.

Dad doesn't have hair and my hair is short, but Holly and Mum have long hair. Mum has (4) ______ hair in the family.

I love swimming. I'm always active – I'm (5) ______ person in the family. I can play the guitar too and I play it loud. I'm (6) ______ member of the family.

I love my family! I think we're (7) ______ family in the world!

▸ Check

16 REVISION After-school plans

Circle the correct answers. *Kreise die richtigen Antworten ein.*

1 Where are / is you going to meet your mum?

2 We're going enjoy / going to enjoy Dungeons & Dragons.

3 The sewing course isn't going to be as easy as / easy than photography.

4 Street dancing is going to be harder than / the hardest activity.

5 I think that this book is going to be more helpful as / helpful than the other book.

6 Who is better than / the best dancer?

7 Knitting is going to be the most interesting / more interesting than activity.

8 We not be going to / aren't going to finish the activity in one day.

☒ 17 REVISION Weekend plans

a) **Complete the first part of the conversation with the phrases in the box.** *Vervollständige den ersten Teil der Unterhaltung mit den Ausdrücken aus dem Kasten.*

are you • as exciting • isn't going • going to • to have • we aren't • what

Leon (1) ________________ are you going to do this weekend?

Carin On Saturday I'm (2) ________________ help my dad in the garden. It isn't going to be (3) ________________ as a day out with you guys, but it (4) ________________ to be bad.

Leon (5) ________________ going to work in the garden on Sunday too?

Carin No, (6) ________________. We're going (7) ________________ Mum's birthday party in our garden!

b) **Complete the rest of the conversation. Write one word in each gap.** *Vervollständige den Rest der Unterhaltung. Schreibe in jede Lücke ein Wort.*

Carin Are you (1) ________________ to do anything fun this weekend?

Leon (2) ________________, we are. My family and I are going (3) ________________ visit London.

Carin (4) ________________ you going to visit famous places?

Leon Yes, I (5) ________________. I'm going to go to the Shard. It's one of the (6) ________________ popular tourist attractions in London. And it's one of (7) ________________ tallest buildings in Western Europe.

Carin Is it taller (8) ________________ the Eiffel Tower?

Leon No, it isn't (9) ________________ tall as that.

The Shard

▶ Check

☒ 18 Revision Question time

Read the answers. Then complete the questions in the going to-future. Add a question word if necessary.
Lies die Antworten. Vervollständige dann die Fragen im going to-future. Ergänze ein Fragewort, falls nötig.

1 Are you going to play ______ computer games this evening? — you / play
No, I'm not. I don't play computer games during the week.

2 ______ open late today? — the school / be
Yes, it is. The school is going to be open late because of the open evening.

3 ______ on holiday this year? — you / go
We're going to go on holiday to Poland.

4 ______ in the competition? — your brother / swim
No, he isn't. He wanted to swim but the coach didn't choose him this time.

5 ______ your homework in the library? — you / do
Because their computers are faster than the one at home.

19 Revision True for you

a) **Write the sentences so they are true for you. Use positive or negative going to-future forms.**
Schreibe Sätze, die auf dich zutreffen. Verwende bejahte und verneinte Formen im going to-future.

1 ______
I / play / tennis / this evening

2 ______
my friends and I / do / after-school activities this year

3 ______
I / cook / for my family this week

4 ______
my friends / come / to my house this weekend

b) **Write sentences about you. Use comparatives and superlatives. Write about the topics below (1–3) and think about your own topic (4).** *Schreibe Sätze über dich. Verwende Komparative und Superlative. Schreibe über die Themen unten (1–3) und überlege dir ein eigenes Thema (4).*

1 My hair (long) ______

2 I'm (tall) ______.

3 My phone (old/fast) ______.

4 ______.

▸ Check

Unit 4
Celebrate!

Erklär-
film

Some / any

Wenn du über eine Menge oder Anzahl sprechen möchtest, du diese Menge oder Anzahl aber nicht genau kennst, verwendest du im Englischen *some* und *any*.

some
- bedeutet „einige", „etwas"
- in bejahten Sätzen
- wenn du um etwas bittest
- wenn du etwas anbietest

Zane invited some friends. (einige Freunde)
Can I have some biscuits, please? (einige Kekse)
Would you like some water? (etwas Wasser)

any
- bedeutet „kein", „keine", „keinen"
- in verneinten Sätzen
- in Fragen

My parents and I don't eat any meat. (kein Fleisch)
Are there any chairs in the classroom? (keine Stühle)

► SB p. 116, p. 206

1 There are some peppers

Look at the pictures and circle the correct words. *Sieh dir die Bilder an und kreise die richtigen Wörter ein.*

1

There's some / any cake.

2

There are some / any fireworks.

3

There aren't some / any tomatoes.

4

There isn't some / any water.

5

There's some / any milk.

6

There aren't some / any lemons.

► Check

ADVANCED

lighthouse 2

Grammarmaster

Lösungen

Cornelsen

Hello again! The last day of the holidays

1 REVISION A day on the beach

1 Sonya **is playing** volleyball. She **isn't swimming**.
2 Josh **isn't standing** on the beach. He**'s surfing**.
3 Ben and his dad **are building** a sandcastle. They **aren't having** a picnic.
4 Justine and her friend **are taking** a photo. They **aren't sleeping**.
5 Holly's dog **isn't eating**. It**'s running** for a ball.

Alle Lösungen aus diesem Heft findest du auch in deiner Cornelsen Lernen App.

Unit 1 Travel and holidays

1 How was your holiday?

Toby How **was** your holiday?
Lucy It **was** great, thanks. We **were** in Spain. **Were** you here in Brighton all the time?
Toby No, we **weren't**. We **were** in Wales for two weeks. It **was** wet and windy. **Was** the weather good in Spain?
Lucy It **was** sunny every day. The weather **was** lovely!

2 The first day back at school

1 **Was** Noah's shirt blue? - No, it **wasn't**. It **was** white.
2 **Was** Sunita's skirt black? - Yes, it **was**.
3 **Were** Noah and Zane's uniforms the same? - Yes, they **were**.

3 Lisa's holiday

My parents were at work, so I **stayed** in Brighton in the holidays. Sunita was in Prague and Alice was in Wales, so it was quiet without my friends. I **visited** my grandma for some days. She's lovely – she lives in Hove.
It's always fun at the beach, so I often **cycled** there in the holidays. I **played** beach volleyball and I **practised** stand up paddling. Sometimes I **watched** a film at the cinema at the Marina.
One night I was at Ravi's birthday party. We **talked**, **listened** to music and **danced**. Poor Ravi! He **worried** about his neighbours.
One weekend my dad and I **travelled** to London. We **tried** to visit all the sights, but there were too many. Dad and I **loved** the city! I **liked** the Pride Parade too. There were 300,000 people in Brighton that day.

4 Irregular verbs

a)
1 was/were • **2** bought • **3** drank • **4** ate • **5** went • **6** met • **7** rode • **8** sat • **9** sang • **10** swam • **11** took • **12** wore
b)
1 were • **2** heard • **3** did • **4** read • **5** rode • **6** bought • **7** ran • **8** sat • **9** forgot • **10** drank • **11** met

5 Lily and Alice's holidays

Lily and her mum **flew** to Poland and **stayed** at her aunt and uncle's house. They **did** lots of different things. One day they **borrowed** her aunt and uncle's bikes and **rode** around Krakow. Lily also **met** the children next door to aunt Svetlana's and they **had** lots of fun in the park.
Alice **went** to Wales with her dad and her brother. It was a long journey – it **took** eight hours! They **were** on a campsite. It **was** a bit cold, but they **loved** it! In the evenings they **cooked** barbecues. Then they **drank** hot chocolate and they **sang** songs by the fire.

6 What about you?

((Lösungsbeispiel))

1 I talked to my grandma this morning.
2 I drank milk for breakfast today.
3 I played the guitar on Tuesday.
4 I ate pizza last weekend.

7 Scout's summer (1)

1 didn't eat • **2** didn't fly • **3** didn't dance • **4** didn't wear • **5** didn't walk • **6** didn't see

8 Mistake or not?

1 We **didn't** go to the football match last week. Was it good?
2 ✓
3 ✓
4 Your teacher didn't **give** you homework last week.
5 ✓
6 It didn't **rain** last weekend.

9 Your last holidays

((Lösungsbeispiel))

On my last holiday my family and I flew to Italy. I bought a cool souvenir for my friend Cem. I didn't play football. But I drew a picture of the beach near our hotel. I swam in the sea too. We didn't cook during the holidays because we got all our meals at the hotel.

10 Revision Scout's summer (2)

Scout wasn't away in the holidays. She **was** in Brighton all summer. She **flew** around the city and she **enjoyed** the good weather. Scout **relaxed** on the beach and she **ate** a lot of food too. There **were** lots of tourists and some of them **gave** their fish and chips to Scout!

11 Revision Reasons why

1 We didn't go to the cinema last weekend because we didn't have time.
2 Ravi didn't visit us last week because he didn't get our invitation.
3 I didn't finish my pizza for lunch because I wasn't hungry.
4 The students weren't in class yesterday because it wasn't a school day.
5 My sisters didn't travel to Brighton yesterday because they didn't feel well.
6 I didn't see the Loch Ness Monster in Scotland because I didn't go to Loch Ness.

Unit 2 Friends and heroes

1 Yes, I did!

a) b)

1 **Did** she **play** football? – **Yes, she did.**
2 **Did** they **walk** to school? – **No, they didn't.**
3 **Did** he **do** the homework? – **Yes, he did.**
4 **Did** we **go** shopping? – **Yes, we did.**
5 **Did** you **get** the train? – **No, I didn't.**
6 **Did** she **swim** in the pool? – **No, she didn't.**

2 The friends' holidays

a)

1 Did Sunita's family visit Prague?
2 Did they stay on a campsite?
3 Did Noah go on holiday to Wales?
4 Did he stay in Brighton?
5 Did Lily travel to Poland?
6 Did she visit her grandparents' house?
7 Did Zane's family go to France?
8 Did their apartment have a pool?

b)

1 Yes, they did.	**7** Yes, they did.	**3** No, he didn't.	**5** Yes, she did.
2 No, they didn't.	**8** Yes, it did.	**4** Yes, he did.	**6** No, she didn't.

3 Did you …?

1 Did you do sport last weekend? – Yes, I did.
2 Did you and your family watch TV last night? – Yes, we did. / No, we didn't.
3 Did you meet your friends at the weekend? – Yes, I did. / No, I didn't.
4 Did you help your parents this morning? – Yes, I did. / No, I didn't.

4 Where did you meet your friends?

1 Where did you meet your friends?
2 Who did Sunita phone last night?
3 What did he have in his lunch box?
4 Why did Emma write a poem?
5 When did you finish your homework?

5 Isla's holiday

1 **Where did** you **go** on holiday?
2 **How long did** you **stay** there?
3 **Who did** you **go** with?
4 **What did** you **do** there?
5 **When did** you **get** home?

6 What they say

Felix says (that) he can do some cool dance moves.
Safira says (that) she loves music.
Leon says (that) this is his new shirt.
Isa says (that) she wants to read her book now.
Lev and Abena say (that) they're/ they are on their way to school.

7 Milo missed the bus

Farah Hi, Milo! What's up?
Milo I'm annoyed **because** I missed the bus.
Farah Oh, no. What happened?
Milo I was a bit late, **so** I ran to High Street. **When** I got to High Street, I heard the bus and I started to run really fast. I waved at the bus driver, but she didn't see me, **so** she closed the doors. The bus drove away **when** I arrived at the bus stop. It's so annoying!

8 Because I can't

1 We can't go to the cinema because we don't have any money.
2 I have lots of homework, so I can't talk for long.
3 Dinner will be ready when you get home.
4 I watch films in English because I want to become better in English.
5 I downloaded his new album, so you can play it in the car.

9 Revision Quiz

a)
1 Where **did** the 2024 Olympic Games take place?
2 Which famous book did Lewis Caroll **write**?
3 Which country **won** the last Eurovision Song Contest?
4 **When** did Germany last **win** the FIFA World Cup?
5 **Which** well-known song **did** DJ Robin & Schürze make in 2022?
6 Who **made** the Avatar films?

b)
1 In France. • **2** Alice in Wonderland. • **3** Sweden (2023). • **4** In 2014. • **5** Layla. •
6 James Cameron.

10 Revision Find the mistakes

1 Where **did** you **go** on holiday? – We went to Belek in Turkey.
2 How did you get to school this morning? – I walked **because** it was a nice day.
3 **Did you start** school late yesterday? – Yes, we did. We started school at 10 a.m.
4 What **did you** buy at the shops? – I bought some clothes.
5 Did you see the cat **when** you got home last night? – No, I didn't.

Unit 3 Activities and games

1 Alma's blog

We**'re going to have** an activity week at our school. There **are going to be** 30 activities and we can choose two. I love sport, so I**'m going to choose** football. Karate sounds good too, but I**'m not going to do** two sports activities. I'd like to try something creative, so I**'m going to try** a screen printing workshop. My friends **aren't going to do** the same as me. Anita **is going to do** chess club and photography. Felix **is going to study** local history and photography. Activity week **is going to be** fun!

2 Activity week plans

1 They'**re/are** going to study local history.
2 I'**m/am** not going to learn karate.
3 She'**s/is** not going to do art.
4 Anita **is** going to try photography.
5 Some activities **are** going to be outdoors.
6 We'**re/are** going to work with animals.

3 You're going to enjoy this!

1 You'**re/are going to enjoy** the zip wire!
2 I'**m not / am not going to go** to a pantomime.
3 She'**s/is going to learn** to cook Thai food.
4 This **is going to be** an insect hotel.
5 We **aren't / are not going to work** with animals.
6 The show **is going to start** at 7.30.
7 They **aren't / are not going to practise** football after school.
8 Thomas **is going to meet** us at the cinema.

4 Jumbled words

1 There aren't going to be teachers.
2 We're going to knit toy animals.
3 He isn't going to plan a summer tea party.
4 We're going to take the school goats for walks.
5 She isn't going to try role-playing games.

5 What are you going to do?

((Lösungsbeispiel))

I'm going to visit my grandma next Saturday. My sister is going to come with me. On Sunday my friends and I are going to watch a film at the cinema. I'm not going to get up early at the weekend.

6 Questions and answers

1 B • **2** D • **3** E • **4** A • **5** C

7 The friends' activity week plans

a) b)

1 Is Zane going to learn about photography? – No, he isn't.
2 Are Lily and Sunita going to do sports activities? – No, they aren't.
3 Is Noah going to study 'History in Brighton'? – No, he isn't.
4 Is Zane going to choose 'Tea party and show'? – Yes, he is.
5 Are Lily and Noah going to do creative activities? – Yes, they are.

8 Missing question words

1 Where • **2** What • **3** When • **4** How

9 Interview questions

a) b)

1	Which activity are you going to choose?	B	Footie Fans.
2	Who is going to plan the activity?	D	Our PE teacher.
3	Where are you going to do the activity?	A	In the park.
4	When is it going to start?	E	Next week.
5	How much is it going cost?	F	It isn't going to cost anything.
6	Why are you going to enjoy it?	C	Because I love football!

10 Superhero quiz

a)

1 Lady Fight • **2** Megastorm • **3** Mr Strong • **4** Captain Right • **5** Dr Heart • **6** Coolboy

b)

((Lösungsbeispiel))

1 Doctor Heart is **nicer** than Lady Fight.
2 Captain Right is **more interesting** than Mr Strong.
3 Megastorm is **more dangerous** than Coolboy.
4 Coolboy is **bigger** than Dr Heart.
5 Mr Strong is **stronger** than Megastorm.
6 Lady Fight is **scarier** than Captain Right.

11 Three superheroes' cars

1 newer than • **2** more beautiful than • **3** faster than • **4** older than • **5** smaller than • **6** more expensive than • **7** more exciting than

12 What's missing?

1 Brighton is **as** warm as London in summer.
2 My sister **is** as old as my best friend.
3 My brother is taller than you. You **aren't** as tall as him.
4 Cars are quicker **than** bikes.
5 My insect hotel isn't as cool **as** the one you made.

13 Holiday places

a)

1 the most expensive • **2** the rainiest • **3** the warmest • **4** the coldest • **5** the most popular

b)

1 Cork and Inverness are popular holiday places, but Brighton is **the most popular** town.
2 Inverness isn't an expensive town. Brighton is more expensive and Cork is **the most expensive** town.
3 Inverness and Cork are warm in summer, but Brighton is **the warmest** town.
4 Cork isn't very cold in winter. Brighton is colder and Inverness is **the coldest** town.
5 Inverness isn't very rainy. Brighton is rainier and Cork is **the rainiest** town.

14 This is the best!

1 the happiest • **2** the worst • **3** the hottest • **4** the noisiest • **5** the most exciting • **6** the best • **7** the most creative • **8** the most beautiful

15 Zane and his family

I'm 12, but I'm not **the youngest** person in my family: my sister Holly is younger. She's seven.
My Dad is 43. He's a bit older than Mum. He's **the oldest** person in the Adebayo family. Mum is 41.
I'm tall, but I'm not **the tallest** person in my family – yet! At the moment Dad is 3 cm taller than me.
Dad doesn't have hair and my hair is short, but Holly and Mum have long hair. Mum has **the longest** hair in the family.
I love swimming. I'm always active – I'm **the most active** person in the family. I can play the guitar too and I play it loud. I'm **the noisiest** member of the family.
I love my family! I think we're **the most wonderful** family in the world!

16 REVISION After-school plans

1 Where **are** you going to meet your mum?
2 We're **going to enjoy** Dungeons & Dragons.
3 The sewing course isn't going to be **as easy as** photography.
4 Street dancing is going to be **the hardest** activity.
5 I think that this book is going to be more **helpful than** the other book.
6 Who is **the best** dancer?
7 Knitting is going to be **the most interesting** activity.
8 We **aren't going to** finish the activity in one day.

☒ 17 REVISION Weekend plans

a)

1 What • 2 going to • 3 as exciting • 4 isn't going • 5 Are you • 6 we aren't • 7 to have

b)

1 going • 2 Yes • 3 to • 4 Are • 5 am • 6 most • 7 the • 8 than • 9 as

☒ 18 REVISION Question time

1 **Are you going to play** computer games this evening?
2 **Is the school going to be** open late today?
3 **Where are you going to go** on holiday this year?
4 **Is your brother going to swim** in the competition?
5 **Why are you going to do** your homework in the library?

19 REVISION True for you

a)

1 I'm going to play / 'm not going to play tennis this evening.
2 My friends and I are going to do / aren't going to do after-school activities this year.
3 I'm going to cook / 'm not going to cook for my family this week.
4 My friends are going to come / aren't going to come to my house this weekend.

b)

((Lösungsbeispiel))

1 My hair is longer than my dad's hair.
2 I'm the tallest student in my class.
3 My phone isn't faster than my friend's phone.
4 My mum is older than my dad.

Unit 4 Celebrate!

1 There are some peppers

1 some • 2 some • 3 any • 4 any • 5 some • 6 any

2 At the supermarket

1 some • 2 some • 3 any • 4 any • 5 some • 6 any

3 Breakfast at the restaurant

1 some • 2 some • 3 some • 4 any • 5 some • 6 any • 7 some • 8 Some

4 What can you see?

((Lösungsbeispiel))

I can see some confetti. I can't see any salad. I can see some cake. And I can see some presents. I can't see any people in the picture.

5 A little or a few?

a little	a few
a little money	*a few apples*
a little music	*a few books*
a little salad	*a few people*
a little sugar	*a few tickets*

6 Planning for a party

1 a little • **2** a few • **3** a little • **4** a few • **5** a few • **6** a few

7 At Emma's party

Lily	Hi, Emma! Is there **anywhere** to put the snacks?
Emma	Yes, just put them on the table over there. Would you like **something** to drink?
Lily	Yes, please. Could I have some juice please?
Emma	Sure. Would you like **something** to eat too?
Lily	Hmm. I don't want **anything** sweet like cake. I think I'd like **something** with vegetables. Is there any salad?
Emma	Sorry, there isn't **anything** with vegetables yet. But there is some fruit salad.
Lily	Fruit salad, great!

8 Later on at Emma's party

1 something • **2** anything • **3** somewhere • **4** anywhere • **5** anybody • **6** somebody

9 The end of Ramadan

a)

Eno Adebayo **has been** a practising Muslim all his life. That's why Eno **has fasted** for the month of Ramadan. Between sunrise and sunset every day during Ramadan, Eno **hasn't had** a drink and he **hasn't eaten** anything. Zane, Holly and their mum Louise **haven't fasted**, but they **have helped** Eno. Soon they are going to celebrate Eid al-Fitr, the end of Ramadan. Zane **has given** invitations to the Eid celebration to his friends. The Adebayos **have celebrated** Eid every year – and Zane and Holly **have received** lots of presents!

b)

regular verbs	irregular verbs
fasted	*been*
helped	*had*
celebrated	*eaten*
received	*given*

10 Jumbled letters

1 arrived • **2** asked • **3** cooked • **4** decided • **5** invited • **6** planned
7 been • **8** bought • **9** come • **10** flown • **11** had • **12** made

11 A few days before Meera and Ben's wedding

Meera and Ben **have decided** to get married. They **have planned** a big wedding near the beach. Ben **has made** a song for Meera. Meera **has invited** Zane and Noah. She **hasn't asked / has not asked** Finn to come to the wedding. Sunita's grandparents **have flown** to the UK from India and her aunt and uncle from Birmingham **have arrived** in Brighton too. Sunita and Willow **haven't bought / have not bought** their wedding clothes, but they are going to go shopping together.

12 We've arrived at Preston Park

Zane	We've arrived at Preston Park.
Finn	Cool! I haven't been / have not been here before.
Lily	Really? I've come / have come here with my family. We've had / have had picnics here.
Noah	Me too. My family and I have been here lots of times.
Zane	I've played / have played football here with my dad.
Finn	I haven't played / have not played football with my dad for a long time. ...

13 Your experiences

1 I have cooked / haven't cooked a meal for my family.
2 I have finished / haven't finished a sudoku.
3 I have driven / haven't driven a car.
4 I have visited / haven't visited another country.
5 I have flown / haven't flown to Africa.
6 I have broken / haven't broken a glass.
7 I have found / I haven't found money on the ground.
8 I have met / I haven't met a famous person.

14 Matching

1 D • **2** F • **3** B • **4** C • **5** A • **6** E

15 Have you ...?

1 **Has** your film **finished**?
2 **Have** they **visited** London?
3 **Has** Tom **tried** Thai food?
4 **Have** you **texted** your friends?
5 **Has** Ms Bond **given** us extra homework?
6 **Have** you **seen** Julia?
7 **Have** I **won** anything?
8 **Have** you **taken** my laptop?

16 Skomer Island

Ben **Have** your parents **decided** where to go on holiday?
Hannah Yes, they **have**. We're going to go to Wales.
Ben Cool. What plans **have** you **made**?
Hannah I don't think we've made any plans. **Have** you ever **visited** Wales?
Ben Yes, I **have**, a few times.
Hannah Where **have** you **been**? What can you do there?
Ben You like birds, right? **Have** you **heard** of Skomer Island?
Hannah No, I **haven't**.
Ben It's a little island. It's an important centre for wildlife – especially birds. **Have** you ever **seen** a puffin?
Hannah No, I **haven't**. Not in real life. ...

17 Questions and answers

1 Have you set the table for dinner? – Yes, I have.
2 Has Paul invited Liz? – Yes, he has.
3 Have you fed your pets? – No, we haven't.
4 Have they prepared for the English text? – Yes, they have.
5 Has Maria left? – No, she hasn't.
6 Have we taken our keys? – Yes, we have

18 Challenge He hasn't ... yet

1 He hasn't been to the library **yet**.
2 Our teacher has **just** told us the news.
3 We haven't met your parents **yet**.
4 They've **already** had breakfast.
5 My sister hasn't arrived home **yet**.
6 Yusseff has **just** chatted with Harry.

19 Challenge I have already ...

1 I**'ve / have already bought** some milk. I went shopping this morning.
2 Sure. I **haven't seen** it **yet** and I've heard it's really good.
3 Yes, I**'ve / have just sent** it to my teacher.
4 No, Holly **has already cleaned** it.

20 Revision Some, any, a little or a few?

1 some • **2** a few • **3** any • **4** a little • **5** some • **6** any

21 Revision Anything good?

1 Someone • **2** something • **3** anywhere • **4** anything • **5** anyone • **6** somewhere

22 REVISION Crossword

								2	
		1	P	L	A	Y	E	D	
			L					E	
	3	M	A	D	E			C	
			N					O	
			N		4			R	
			E		G			A	
5	H	A	D		O			T	
			6	S	T	O	L	E	N
								D	

23 REVISION Have you visited England?

1 anywhere • **2** been • **3** Where • **4** have • **5** some • **6** seen • **7** a few • **8** have • **9** haven't • **10** haven't

24 REVISION Have you ever ...?

a) b)

1 Have you celebrated Eid al-Fitr? – Yes, I have. / No, I haven't.
2 Has your mum bought a cool car? – Yes, she has. / No, she hasn't.
3 Has your best friend given you a birthday present? – Yes, he/she has. / No, he/she hasn't.
4 Has your grandma written a song? – Yes, she has. / No, she hasn't.
5 Have you eaten Sushi? – Yes, I have. / No, I haven't.

Unit 5 Getting ready for the future

1 Future jobs

a) b)

1 'll work • **2** won't be • **3** 'll work • **4** 'll / will • **5** won't • **6** 'll / will

2 I think it'll be ...

1 It won't rain tomorrow. I think it'll be sunny.
2 My sister won't / will not be at home later. I'm sure she'll / will go out with her friends.
3 Varndean won't / will not lose the match on Saturday. I'm sure they'll / will win.
4 Mum's new job will be fun. I bet it won't / will not be boring!

3 Lily says

1 I **won't play** tennis this weekend. **I'll play** in the park.
2 Mum and I **will go** to Poland. We **won't / will not go** on holiday to Germany.
3 Chloe's cat **will lie** on the sofa. It **won't / will not lie** in Chloe's garden.
4 **I'll / will draw** some manga characters. I **won't / will not draw** real people.
5 Chloe is 23 now. She**'ll / will be** 24 next year. She **won't / will not be** 25.
6 My dad **won't / will not drive** a bus tomorrow. He**'ll / will drive** a van.

4 Fifty years from now

1 E • **2** A • **3** B • **4** D • **5** C

5 Will you ...?

1 **Will** you go to the park this weekend? – Yes, I will. / No, I won't.
2 **Will** you get a job next summer? – Yes, I will. / No, I won't.
3 **Will** you watch TV in the evening? – Yes, I will. / No, I won't.
4 **Will** you see your grandparents this week? – Yes, I will. / No, I won't.
5 **Will** you ride your bike to school tomorrow? – Yes, I will. / No, I won't.

6 Question words

1 Where • **2** What • **3** Who • **4** How • **5** What

7 Tim's dream job

a)
1 Will you work
2 Will you use
3 Will you and your colleagues need
4 Where will your office be?
5 Will your job be
6 When will you work

b)
Tim will be a **musician**.

8 Adverbs of manner

1 beautifully • **2** clearly • **3** fast • **4** well • **5** happily • **6** hard • **7** loudly • **8** nervously • **9** quietly • **10** terribly

9 Adverb or adjective?

1 We worked **hard** in the garden today. – Yes, I didn't know gardening was hard!
2 That's a fast car! – It's going to go past us really **fast** now, look!
3 He's talking **nervously**. But why is he nervous?
4 This is a very quiet cafe. – Yes, there's no music and everyone is speaking **quietly**.
5 I did **well** in my maths exam. – I agree, B+ is a very good mark!
6 Why do you have to play your music so **loudly**? – Because I love loud music!

10 Parts of speech

1 a mechanic: Objekt • **2** went: Verb • **3** next week: Zeitangabe • **4** Mum: Subjekt • **5** at my house: Ortsangabe; at 8.30: Zeitangabe

11 My aunt's new cafe

1 My aunt wants to open a cafe at the beach next month.
2 So she has a lot of things to prepare at the cafe every day.
3 She arrives at the beach at 7 a.m.
4 Then she works very hard in her cafe every day.
5 She comes home late every night.

12 Ordering

1 I wasn't at the supermarket yesterday.
2 On Saturdays I stay in bed until 10 o'clock.
3 After dinner we helped Mum and Dad in the kitchen.
4 I'll babysit my little cousin at my grandma's house this weekend.
5 She works for an animal charity during the holidays.
6 They'd like to invite us to a clean-up in our neighbourhood.

13 Our jobs at home

1 My sister **rarely** takes out the rubbish.
2 She **always** empties the dishwasher.
3 I **often** vacuum the floor in my room.
4 We **sometimes** clean the garage with Dad.
5 It's **always** fun to look after our pets.
6 We **often** fold clean clothes.
7 My brother is **sometimes** in the garden with Mum at the weekend.

14 Challenge What will happen if ...?

1 B • 2 E • 3 D • 4 C • 5 A

15 Challenge At the charity shop

Joana Look at all the cool video games in here, Mum! Can I buy one?
Mum If you **buy** a video game, **will you have** enough money for Dad's birthday present?
Joana I have £10. The games are £4.50. So **I'll have** £5.50 for Dad's present if I **get** a game. What should I do, Mum?
Mum If you **aren't** sure, maybe it **will be** best to check out how much the other things in here are.
Joana OK. If I **find** something for Dad that isn't too expensive, **I'll get** one of these video games too.

Five minutes later ...

Joana Dad wouldn't like anything in here, only the video games. But I have a fantastic idea! If I **buy** two video games, one for me and one for Dad, **I'll have** a great present for him. And **I'll play** two different games if I **borrow** Dad's game!

16 Revision Talking about jobs

Ms Bond This afternoon **we'll / will talk** about jobs you'd like to do one day. Liam, what **will you do** when you're older? **Will you be** a teacher like me?
Liam I love school, but I **won't / will not work** in a school when I'm older. I think I'**ll / will get** a job as a nurse.
Ms Bond I'm sure you'**ll / will be** a brilliant nurse, Liam.
Liam Thank you.
Ms Bond Emma, what about you?
Emma I love art so I think I'**ll / will become** an artist. **Will I have to** go to university to be an artist?
Ms Bond No, some artists go to university and some don't. I think you'**ll / will love** university! But don't worry, you **won't / will not need** to think about university until you're much older.

17 REVISION Jumbled sentences

1 We won't / will not go to our judo lesson tomorrow.
2 Will you be at the football match on Saturday?
3 What will you do next weekend?
4 Peter will meet his friends at the youth club this afternoon.
5 Maye I'll / will become an architect one day.
6 Will Mum and Dad wait for us at school at 3 o'clock?

18 REVISION What will you do?

((Lösungsbeispiel))
I think I'll live in a different country. Maybe I'll become a nurse. I won't become a police officer. I'll have a big family. I'm sure I'll have a dog, but I won't have a fast car.

19 REVISION Adverbs

1 quickly • **2** nervous • **3** terribly • **4** fast • **5** clear

20 REVISION How did they speak or act?

1 'I love animals. I hope I'll be a vet one day!' said Noah **excitedly** and he smiled.
2 'Lily sang **beautifully** on the way to school,' said Ava.
3 'I want to play football. But where's my ball?' shouted Zane **angrily**.
4 'I didn't do **well** in the exams last week. I'll study harder next term,' said Lily.
5 'My bike isn't fast,' said Alice. 'Can we ride more **slowly**, please?'

2 At the supermarket

Emma is at the supermarket. Look at her shopping list and complete her sentences with *some* or *any*.
Emma ist im Supermarkt. Schau dir ihre Einkaufsliste an und vervollständige ihre Sätze mit some *oder* any.

Right. I have (1) some *flour and I have (2)________ sugar. I don't have (3)________ bananas and I don't have (4)________ chocolate. I have (5)________ yoghourt, but there aren't (6)________ eggs.*

Shopping List

- [x] ~~flour~~
- [x] ~~yoghurt~~
- [ ] eggs
- [ ] chocolate
- [x] ~~sugar~~
- [ ] bananas

3 Breakfast at the restaurant

Read the conversation and complete it with *some* or *any*.
Lies die Unterhaltung und vervollständige sie mit some *oder* any.

Waiter[1] Good morning. Would you like (1)__________ juice?

Elias Yes, please. And can my sister have (2)__________ water, please?

Waiter Of course. Would you like (3)__________ toast?

Elias Yes, please, but we don't need (4)__________ butter. We'd just like (5)__________ cheese, please.

Waiter I'm sorry, there isn't (6)__________ cheese. But we have (7)__________ ham.

Elias (8) __________ ham would be perfect, thank you!

4 What can you see?

Look at the picture and write five sentences about what you can see and what you can't see. Use *some* and *any*. *Schau dir das Bild an und schreibe fünf Sätze darüber, was du sehen und was du nicht sehen kannst. Verwende* some *und* any.

I can see some confetti. I can't see any salad.

____

____

____

____

► Check

[1] **waiter** *der Kellner*

Erklärfilm

A little / a few

Du weißt schon, wie du über große Mengen sprechen kannst. Du verwendest dafür *much* für nicht zählbare Dinge und *many* für zählbare Dinge. Möchtest du aber über kleine Mengen sprechen, verwendest du a little und a few.

a little
- bedeutet „ein wenig", „etwas"
- bei nicht zählbaren Nomen, das heißt, du kannst von diesen Nomen keinen Plural bilden *(water, juice, music, love, money)*

I need a little fruit for my cake. (ein wenig Obst)
Can I have a little sugar for my tea, please? (etwas Zucker)

a few
- bedeutet „einige", „ein paar"
- bei zählbaren Nomen, das heißt, du kannst einen Plural bilden *(one apple, two apples)*

There were a few mistakes in your test. (einige Fehler)
There are only a few strawberries left. (ein paar Erdbeeren)

► SB p. 116, p. 206

5 A little or a few?

Write the words from the box into the right list. Write them with *a little* and *a few*.
Schreibe die Wörter aus dem Kasten in die richtige Liste. Schreibe sie mit a little *und* a few.

apples • books • ~~money~~ • music • people • salad • sugar • tickets

a little	a few
a little money	

6 Planning for a party

Read the conversation and complete it with *a little* and *a few*.
Lies die Unterhaltung und vervollständige sie mit a little *und* a few.

Lily What can we take to Emma's party?
Finn We could take (1)____________ food.
Lily Good idea. I can take (2)____________ snacks.
Sunita And I can make (3)____________ lemonade!
Noah My mum is going to make (4)____________ pizzas.
Lily That sounds great. What about music?
Zane I can play (5)____________ songs on my guitar if you like?
And I can bring (6)____________ games too.

► Check

Zusammensetzungen mit *some* und *any*

Some verwendest du vor allem in bejahten Aussagesätzen, *any* findest du überwiegend in verneinten Aussagesätzen und in Fragen.

Dieselbe Regel gilt auch für Zusammensetzungen mit *some* und *any*.

- In bejahten Aussagesätzen: *somebody/someone, something, somewhere*
  There's somebody in the house. (Da ist jemand im Haus.)
  I can do something nice for my mum. (Ich kann etwas Schönes für meine Mutter machen.)
  My friend is somewhere in the classroom. (Mein Freund ist irgendwo im Klassenraum.)
- In verneinten Aussagesätzen und Fragen: *anybody/anyone, anything, anywhere*
  Is there anybody at school today? (Ist heute jemand in der Schule?)
  There isn't anything to eat! (Es gibt nichts zu essen.)
  Can you see my phone anywhere? (Kannst du irgendwo mein Telefon sehen?)

▶ SB p. 123, p. 208

7 At Emma's party

Read the conversation and circle the correct words.
Lies die Unterhaltung und kreise die richtigen Wörter ein.

Lily Hi, Emma! Is there anywhere / anything to put the snacks?

Emma Yes, just put them on the table over there. Would you like something / somebody to drink?

Lily Yes, please. Could I have some juice please?

Emma Sure. Would you like somewhere / something to eat too?

Lily Hmm. I don't want anything / anybody sweet like cake.
I think I'd like somebody / something with vegetables. Is there any salad?

Emma Sorry, there isn't anything / anywhere with vegetables yet. But there's some fruit salad.

Lily Fruit salad, great!

Wenn du mit einer Frage etwas anbietest oder um etwas bittest, verwendest du *some, somebody/someone, something, somewhere*:

Would you like something to drink? (Möchtest du etwas zu trinken?)

8 Later on at Emma's party

Complete the sentences with the words on the right. *Vervollständige die Sätze mit den Wörtern rechts.*

Finn Is there (1)____________ I can help you with, Emma?
Emma No, thanks. There isn't (2)____________ to do.

anything | something

Noah Let's go (3)____________ quiet. It's noisy here.
Emma Sorry, there isn't (4)____________ quiet.

anywhere | somewhere

Zane Did (5)____________ see my guitar? I need (6)____________ to tell me where I can find it.

anybody | somebody

▶ Check

Erklär-film

Das present perfect: Bejahte und verneinte Aussagesätze

Mit dem *present perfect* sagst du, dass jemand irgendwann etwas getan hat oder dass irgendwann etwas geschehen ist. Der genaue Zeitpunkt des Geschehens ist unwichtig oder unbekannt.

Das *present perfect* besteht aus zwei Teilen:

I/you/we/they	have / haven't	+	3. Form des Verbs
he/she/it	has / hasn't		(Partizip Perfekt; Englisch: past participle)

Das past participle bildest du so:

- Bei regelmäßigen Verben hängst du -ed an den Infinitiv an, z. B.

play + ed → played — *We've played basketball a lot of times.*

visit + ed → visited — *Mara hasn't visited Brighton.*

- Bei unregelmäßigen Verben musst du die 3. Form lernen, z. B.

be → been — *Ahmet has been to Scotland very often.*

do → done — *I've done my homework.*

have → had — *My parents haven't had a car.*

► SB p. 119, p. 207, pp. 312–313

9 The end of Ramadan

a) **Read the text about Zane's dad. Circle the correct form of *have*.**
Lies den Text über Zanes Vater. Kreise die richtige Form von have *ein.*

Eno Adebayo **has / have** been a practising Muslim all his life. That's why Eno **has / have** fasted for the month of Ramadan. Between sunrise and sunset every day during Ramadan, Eno **hasn't / haven't** had a drink and he **hasn't / haven't** eaten anything. Zane, Holly and their mum Louise **hasn't / haven't** fasted, but they **has / have** helped Eno. Soon they are going to celebrate Eid al-Fitr, the end of Ramadan. Zane **has / have** given invitations to the Eid celebration to his friends. The Adebayos **has / have** celebrated Eid every year – and Zane and Holly **has / have** received lots of presents!

b) **Look at the past participles in a. Put them into the right list.**
Schaue dir die 3. Form der Verben in a an. Trage sie in die richtige Liste ein.

regular verbs	irregular verbs
	been

► Check

10 Jumbled letters

Put the letters in the correct order to form past participles. You can use the irregular verb pages in your Student's book for help (pages 312–313). *Bringe die Buchstaben in die richtige Reihenfolge, um die 3. Form des Verbs zu bilden. Wenn du Hilfe brauchst, kannst du die unregelmäßigen Verben in deinem Schulbuch nachschlagen (Seiten 312–313).*

	regular verbs		
	infinitive	simple past	past participle
1	arrive	arrived	arrived
2	ask	asked	
3	cook	cooked	
4	decide	decided	
5	invite	invited	
6	plan	planned	
	irregular verbs		
	infinitive	simple past	past participle
7	be	was/were	been
8	buy	bought	
9	come	came	
10	fly	flew	
11	have	had	
12	make	made	

~~v a r d r i e~~
d e a s k
d o c k e o
c i d d e d e
v i n t e d i
n e d p n l a

~~n e b e~~
t g o h b u
m o c e
n o w f l
d a h
m d a e

Das *past participle* bildest du bei regelmäßigen Verben genauso wie das *simple past* mit *-ed*. Beachte:
1 Ein stummes *e* fällt weg.
2 Nach einem einzelnen, betonten Vokal wird der Konsonant verdoppelt.
3 Ein *y* nach Konsonant wird zu *ied*.

11 A few days before Meera and Ben's wedding

Complete the sentences. Use the positive (+) or negative (–) present perfect of the verbs in exercise 10. *Vervollständige die Sätze. Verwende bejahte (+) oder verneinte (–) Formen der Verben aus Übung 10 im present perfect.*

Meera and Ben (1) have decided ____________ (decide +) to get married. They (2) ____________ (plan +) a big wedding near the beach. Ben (3) ____________ (make +) a song for Meera. Meera (4) ____________ (invite +) Zane and Noah. She (5) ____________ (ask –) Finn to come to the wedding. Sunita's grandparents (6) ____________ (fly +) to the UK from India and her aunt and uncle from Birmingham (7) ____________ (arrive +) in Brighton too. Sunita and Willow (8) ____________ (buy –) their wedding clothes, but they're going to go shopping together.

▸ Check

12 We've arrived at Preston Park

Write the conversation. Use the present perfect.
Schreibe die Unterhaltung auf. Verwende das present perfect.

Kurzformen:
have → I've lived
has → he's gone
have not → we haven't seen
has not → she hasn't read

Zane We've arrived at Preston Park.
we / arrive / at Preston Park

Finn Cool! ______________________.
I / not be / here before

Lily Really? ______________________.
I / come / here with my family

______________________.
we / have / picnics here

Noah Me too. ______________________.
my family and I / be / here lots of times

Zane ______________________
______________________.
I / play / football here with my dad

Finn ______________________
______________________.
I / not play / football with my dad for a long time

Zane Don't worry, Finn. Dad and I are going to come here next weekend. Why don't you come with us?

Preston Park

13 Your experiences

Write what you have or haven't done. *Schreibe, was du gemacht und was du nicht gemacht hast.*

1 cook / a meal for my family — I haven't cooked a meal for my family.
2 finish / a sudoku ______________________
3 drive / a car ______________________
4 visit / another country ______________________
5 fly / to Africa ______________________
6 break / a glass ______________________
7 find / money on the ground ______________________
8 meet / a famous person ______________________

► Check

Erklär-film

Das present perfect: Fragen und Kurzantworten

Entscheidungsfragen im *present perfect* beginnen mit *Have* oder *Has*.

Have you finished your homework? – Yes, I have. / No, I haven't.
Has Louisa met Paolo? – Yes, she has. / No, she hasn't.

▶ SB p. 121, p. 208

14 Matching

Match the questions and answers and write the right letters A–F in the boxes.
Ordne die Fragen und Antworten zu und schreibe die richtigen Buchstaben A–F in die Kästchen.

1 Have you found your classroom?
2 Has the rain stopped?
3 Has your sister taken her judo test?
4 Have you seen my pen anywhere?
5 Have they left the cinema?
6 Has Leon played the violine?

A No, they haven't. They're still there.
B Yes, she has. She has the green belt now.
C Yes, I have. It's on the table.
D Yes, we have. It's room 11.
E No, he hasn't. But he wants to learn how to play it.
F Yes, it has. It's sunny now.

1 ☐ 2 ☐ 3 ☐ 4 ☐ 5 ☐ 6 ☐

15 Have you …?

Write questions. *Schreibe Fragen.*

1 *Has* your film *finished* (finish)? – No, it hasn't.
2 ______ they ______ London (visit)? – Yes, they have.
3 ______ Tom ______ Thai food (try)? – Yes, he has.
4 ______ you ______ your friends (text)? – No, we haven't.
5 ______ Ms Bond ______ us extra homework (give)? – No, she hasn't.
6 ______ you ______ Julia (see)? – Yes, I have.
7 ______ I ______ anything (win)? – Yes, you have.
8 ______ you ______ my laptop (take)? – No, I haven't.

▶ Check

16 Skomer Island

Read the conversation. Complete the questions and short answers. Use the verbs from the box. *Lies die Unterhaltung. Vervollständige die Fragen und Kurzantworten. Verwende die Verben aus dem Kasten.*

Bei einer Frage mit Fragewort steht das Fragewort am Satzanfang
What have you heard?
Where have you been?

be • ~~decide~~ • hear • make • see • visit

Ben *Have* ______ your parents *decided* ______ where to go on holiday?

Hannah Yes, they ______. We're going to go to Wales.

Ben Cool. What plans ______ you ______?

Hannah I don't think we've made any plans. ______ you ever ______ Wales?

Ben Yes, I ______, a few times.

Hannah Where ______ you ______? What can you do there?

Ben You like birds, right? ______ you ______ of Skomer Island?

Hannah No, I ______.

Ben It's a little island. It's an important centre for wildlife – especially birds. ______ you ever ______ a puffin?

Hannah No, I ______. Not in real life.

Ben Ask your parents if you can visit Skomer Island then. There are lots of puffins on Skomer.

Puffins on Skomer Island

17 Questions and answers

Write present perfect questions and complete the short answers.
Schreibe Fragen im present perfect und vervollständige die Kurzantworten.

1 ______ Yes, I ______.
you / set / the table for dinner?

2 ______ Yes, he ______.
Paul / invite / Liz?

3 ______ No, we ______.
you / feed / your pets?

4 ______ Yes, they ______.
they / prepare / for the English test?

5 ______ No, she ______.
Maria / leave?

6 ______ Yes, we ______.
we / take / our keys?

► Check

Challenge: Das present perfect mit unbestimmten Zeitangaben

Das *present perfect* verwendest du mit unbestimmten Zeitangaben. Beachte die Stellung im Satz:

already	schon, bereits	*Dad has already bought flowers for Mum.*
just	gerade (eben), soeben	*I've just talked to him.*
not ... yet	noch nicht	*I haven't eaten yet.*

► SB p. 141

18 Challenge He hasn't ... yet

Write the word in the right place in the sentence. *Schreibe das Wort an der richtigen Stelle im Satz.*

1 He hasn't ________ been to the library *yet* ________. — yet

2 Our teacher has ________ told us the news ________. — just

3 We haven't ________ met your parents ________. — yet

4 They've ________ had breakfast ________. — already

5 My sister hasn't ________ arrived home ________. — yet

6 Yusseff has ________ chatted with Harry ________. — just

19 Challenge I have already ...

Complete the sentences with the present perfect of the verbs in the box and the time phrases.
Vervollständige die Sätze mit dem present perfect der Verben im Kasten sowie den Zeitangaben.

already / buy • already / clean • just / send • not see / yet

Noah Do we have any milk or did we finish it yesterday?
Dad I (1)________ ________ ________ some milk. I went shopping this morning.

Alice Have you seen the new Star Wars film? Would you like to go and see it?
Finn Sure. I (2)________ ________ it ________ and I've heard it's really good.

Mum Have you finished your homework, Lily?
Lily Yes, I (3)________ ________ ________ it to my teacher.

Dad Have you cleaned the bathroom?
Zane No, Holly (4)________ ________ ________ it.

► Check

20 Revision Some, any, a little or a few?

Read the family's sentences. Circle the right words.
Lies die Sätze der Familienmitglieder. Kreise die richtigen Wörter ein.

1 I've just eaten some / a few chocolate.
2 Can I eat a little / a few of your sausages?
3 There aren't any / some apples on the table.
4 Could I have a little / a few more juice, please?
5 There's a few / some bread.
6 Dad doesn't like any / a few bananas.

21 Revision Anything good?

Complete the sentences. *Vervollständige die Sätze.*

anyone • anything • anywhere • someone • something • somewhere

1 ______________________________ has taken my money!
2 I'm going to tell you ______________________________, but it's a secret.
3 Can you think of ______________________________ fun to go to this weekend?
4 I don't want to do ______________________________ this evening.
5 Has ______________________________ seen my phone?
6 I would like to travel ______________________________ really far away.

22 Revision Crossword

Fill the crossword with the past participles of the verbs.
Vervollständige das Kreuzworträtsel mit der 3. Form der Verben.

Across →
1 I haven't (play) this song.
3 Have you (make) the cake?
5 Lily has (have) lunch.
6 Someone has (steal) my bag!

Down ↓
1 The class has (plan) their next trip.
2 Has Marc (decorate) the room?
4 Peter has (get) a good mark in his maths test.

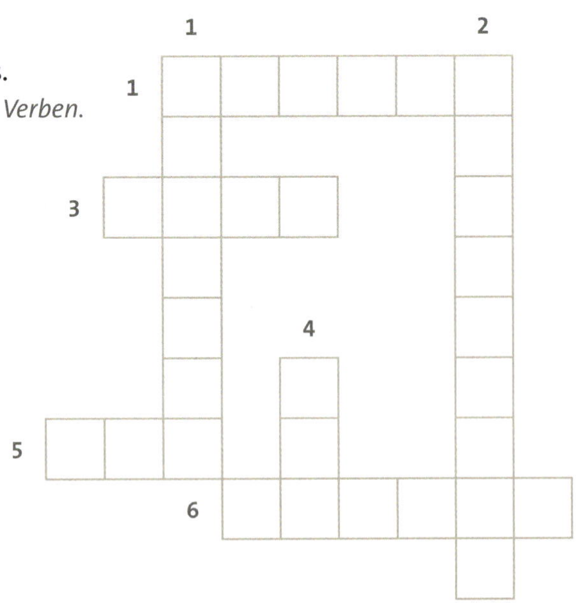

▸ Check

23 REVISION Have you visited England?

Read the conversation about a trip to England. Complete the sentences with the words in the box. *Lies die Unterhaltung über eine Reise nach England. Vervollständige die Sätze mit den Wörtern aus dem Kasten.*

a few • anywhere • been • have • Have • haven't (2x) • seen • some • Where

Jacob Have you travelled (1)_______________ outside Germany?

Olivia Yes, I have. I've (2)_______________ to England.

Jacob Cool. (3)_______________ have you been to?

Olivia I (4)_______________ visited Oxford.

Jacob Oxford! Is Oxford nice?

Olivia Yes, it is. There are (5)_______________ amazing old buildings and …

Christ Church College

Jacob Hey! Have you (6)_______________ Christ Church College? They filmed (7)_______________ of the scenes in Harry Potter there!

Olivia Yes, I (8)_______________. It was amazing!

Jacob What about fish and chips? I (9)_______________ tried British fish and chips before. Have you?

Olivia No, I (10)_______________. Next time!

24 REVISION Have you ever …?

a) **Write present perfect questions.** *Schreibe Fragen im present perfect.*

1 you / celebrate / Eid al Fitr / ?

_______________________________________ _______________

2 your mum / buy / a cool car / ?

_______________________________________ _______________

3 your best friend / give / you / a birthday present / ?

_______________________________________ _______________

4 your grandma / write / a song / ?

_______________________________________ _______________

5 you / eat / Sushi / ?

_______________________________________ _______________

b) **Now write your short answers.** *Schreibe nun deine Kurzantworten.*

▸ Check

Unit 5
Getting ready for the future

Erklär-
film

Das will-future: Bejahte und verneinte Aussagesätze

Du verwendest das *will-future*, wenn du sagen willst, was in der Zukunft wahrscheinlich geschehen wird. Oft verwendest du es mit *I think, maybe, I'm sure*.

A **Bejahte Aussagesätze**

I / you / he / she / it / we / you / they	will / 'll	+ infinitive	*I think we'll stay at home tomorrow.* *It'll be rainy.*

B **Verneinte Aussagesätze**

I / you / he / she / it / we / you / they	will not / won't	+ infinitive	*I'm sure I won't become a programmer.*

▸ SB p. 148, p. 209

1 Future jobs

Look at the pictures. What are the Varndean students' future job plans?
Schau dir die Bilder an. Welche Berufspläne haben die Kinder von Varndean?

a) **Circle the correct words.** *Kreise die richtigen Wörter ein.*

1

In the future, I 'll work / won't work for an animal charity.

2

I 'll be / won't be a police officer.

3

I think I 'll work / won't work as a vet.

b) **Complete the sentences with *will/'ll* or *won't*.** *Vervollständige die Sätze mit* will/'ll *oder* won't.

4

I hope I ______________ be a professional gamer.

5

Maybe I ______________ become a professional footballer.

6

I'm sure I ______________ work as a programmer.

▸ Check

2 I think it'll be …

Write pairs of will-future sentences. Use short forms.
Schreibe Satzpaare im will-future. Verwende die Kurzformen.

1 It / not rain / tomorrow. / I think it / be / sunny.
It won't rain tomorrow. I think it'll be sunny.

2 My sister / not be / at home later. / I'm sure she / go / out with her friends.
____

3 Varndean / not lose / the match on Saturday. / I'm sure they / win.
____

4 Mum's new job / be / fun. / I bet it / not be / boring!
____

3 Lily says

Look at the pictures and complete Lily's sentences with *will/'ll / won't* and the verbs in the box.
Sieh dir die Bilder an und vervollständige Lilys Sätze mit will/'ll / won't *und den Verben aus dem Kasten.*

be • draw • drive • go • lie • ~~play~~

I won't play tennis this weekend. I 'll play in the park.

Mum and I ____________ to Poland. We ____________ on holiday to Germany.

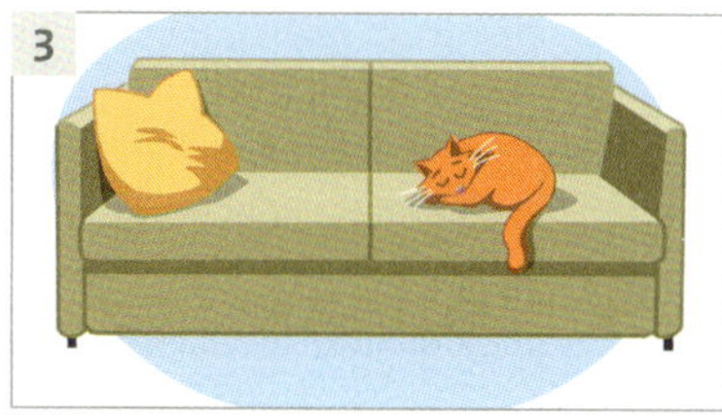

Chloe's cat ____________ on the sofa. It ____________ in Chloe's garden.

I ____________ some manga characters. I ____________ real people.

Chloe is 23 now. She ____________ 24 next year. She ____________ 25.

My dad ____________ a bus tomorrow. He ____________ a van.

▸ Check

Erklär-film

Das will-future: Fragen und Kurzantworten

Bei Fragen im *will-future* steht *will* am Satzanfang. Hat die Frage ein Fragewort, steht das noch davor.

Will your sister be at the party? – Yes, she will.

Will you meet Oscar tomorrow? – No, I won't.

When will she arrive? – At 8 o'clock.

Where will we meet? – In front of the cinema.

▸ SB p. 148, p. 209

4 Fifty years from now

Match the questions and answers and write the right letters A–E in the boxes.

Ordne die Fragen und Antworten zu und schreibe die richtigen Buchstaben A–E in die Kästchen.

1 What will jobs be like?

2 How will people travel around?

3 What will the weather be like?

4 Will robots teach in schools?

5 Will we do the chores at home?

A I think people will have flying cars.

B Maybe it'll be hotter, but wetter.

C We'll do some, but robots will cook and make beds.

D No, they won't. Schools will have real teachers!

E I'm sure everyone will use computers in their jobs.

1 ☐ 2 ☐ 3 ☐ 4 ☐ 5 ☐

5 Will you …?

Complete the questions and answers with *will, won't, yes* or *no*.

Vervollständige die Fragen und Antworten mit will, won't, yes *oder* no.

1 ____________ you go to the park this weekend? – ________________, I ________________.

2 ____________ you get a job next summer? – ________________, I ________________.

3 ____________ you watch TV in the evening? – ________________, I ________________.

4 ____________ you see your grandparents this week? – ________________, I ________________.

5 ____________ you ride your bike to school tomorrow? – ________________, I ________________.

▸ Check

6 Question words

Complete the questions. Use *How, What, Where* or *Who*.
Vervollständige die Fragen. Verwende How, What, Where *oder* Who.

1 ____________ will you go on holiday this summer?

– I don't know. My parents haven't talked about where we want to go.

2 ____________ will you read next?

– I'm not sure what I'll read next. Do you know a good book?

3 ____________ will you invite to your party?

– I haven't invited anyone yet. Would you like to come?

4 ____________ will you get to the park?

– I think I'll ride my bike.

5 ____________ will you have for lunch today?

– I'm not sure. Maybe some soup.

7 Tim's dream job

a) **Complete the interview questions with the words in brackets.**
Vervollständige die Interviewfragen mit den Wörtern in Klammern.

Alisha (1) Will you work ____________ (you /work) with people?

Tim Yes, I will. I'll work with people and for people.

Alisha (2) ____________ (you / use) computers?

Tim No, I won't. But some of my colleagues will use them.

Alisha (3) ____________ (you and your colleagues / need) a car?

Tim Yes, we'll need a car to travel with all our instruments.

Alisha (4) ____________ (where / your office / be)?

Tim I won't have an office. I'll work in clubs, concert halls, maybe in stadiums too.

Alisha (5) ____________ (your job / be) fun?

Tim Oh, yes! I hope it will be lots of fun.

Alisha (6) ____________ (when / you / work), at day or at night?

Tim At day and at night. I'll practise during the day and I'll work in the evenings.

b) Challenge **What's Tim's dream job?** *Was ist Tims Traumberuf?*

Tim will be a ____________.

► Check

Adverbien der Art und Weise

Adverbien der Art und Weise beziehen sich auf ein Verb. Sie drücken aus, wie jemand etwas tut oder wie etwas geschieht:

She walked home slowly.
(Sie ging langsam nach Hause.)

"Oh, yes!" he said excitedly.
(„Oh ja!", sagte er aufgeregt.)

Die meisten Adverbien der Art und Weise bildest du, indem du -ly an das Adjektiv anhängst:

slow + ly → slowly

excited + ly → excitedly

!
- *-y + -ly → -ily: angry → angrily*
- *-le + -ly → -ly: horrible → horribly*
- Das Adverb zu *good* heißt *well*.
- Bei *fast* und *hard* haben Adjektiv und Adverb dieselbe Form.

► SB p. 155, p. 209

8 Adverbs of manner

Write the adverbs. *Schreibe die Adverbien.*

1 beautiful ______________________

2 clear ______________________

3 fast ______________________

4 good ______________________

5 happy ______________________

6 hard ______________________

7 loud ______________________

8 nervous ______________________

9 quiet ______________________

10 terrible ______________________

9 Adverb or adjective?

Circle the adverb in each pair of sentences. *Kreise das Adverb in jedem Satzpaar ein.*

1 We worked hard in the garden today.
– Yes, I didn't know gardening was hard!

2 That's a fast car!
– It's going to go past us really fast now, look!

3 He's talking nervously. – But why is he nervous?

4 This is a very quiet cafe. – Yes, there's no music and everyone is speaking quietly.

5 I did well in my maths exam. – I agree, B+ is a very good mark!

6 Why do you have to play your music so loudly? – Because I love loud music!

Nach *be* steht immer ein Adjektiv:
Ann is pretty.

► Check

Die Wortstellung

Im englischen Aussagesatz ist die Wortstellung immer subject – verb – object: *I meet my friends.*

Eine Ortsangabe steht meist nach Verb und Objekt.

Subjekt	Verb	Objekt	Ort
I	*meet*	*my friends*	*at school.*

Zeitangaben stehen am Anfang oder am Ende des Satzes.

Zeit	Subjekt	Verb	Objekt	Zeit
Every day	*I*	*meet*	*my friends.*	
	I	*meet*	*my friends*	*every day.*

Stehen in einem Satz eine Orts- und eine Zeitangabe, kommt Ort vor Zeit.
Das ist wie im Alphabet: O kommt vor Z.

	Ort	Zeit
I meet my friends	*at school*	*every day.*

► SB p. 155, p. 210

10 Parts of speech

Read the sentences. What are the phrases in blue? *Lies die Sätze. Was sind die Satzglieder in Blau?*

1 I won't be a mechanic. — a mechanic: (Objekt) / Subjekt

2 They went for a bike ride yesterday. — went: Verb / Zeitangabe

3 It's my birthday next week. — next week: Ortsangabe / Zeitangabe

4 Mum is going to help us tomorrow. — Mum: Objekt / Subjekt

5 I'll meet you at my house at 8.30. — at my house: Objekt / Ortsangabe; at 8.30: Ortsangabe / Zeitangabe

11 My aunt's new cafe

Write the sentence parts in the right place. *Schreibe die Satzteile an die richtige Stelle im Satz.*

1 My aunt wants to open a cafe ______________________ — at the beach / next month

2 So she has a lot of things to prepare ______________________ — every day / at the cafe

3 She arrives ______________________ — at 7 a.m. / at the beach

4 Then she works very hard ______________________ — in her cafe / every day

5 She comes ______________________ — late every night / home

► Check

12 Ordering

Write sentences. Put the words in the right order.
Schreibe Sätze. Bringe die Wörter in die richtige Reihenfolge.

1 at the supermarket / I / yesterday. / wasn't
I wasn't at the supermarket yesterday.

2 in bed / stay / On Saturdays / I / until 10 o'clock.
____

3 After dinner / we / Mum and Dad / in the kitchen. / helped
____

4 my little cousin / I / at my grandma's house / 'll babysit / this weekend.
____

5 She / for an animal charity / works / during the holidays.
____

6 in our neighbourhood. / us / 'd like to invite / They / to a clean-up
____

13 Our jobs at home

Write the sentences with the adverbs of frequency in the correct place.
Schreibe die Sätze mit den Häufigkeitsadverbien an der richtigen Stelle.

1 My sister takes out the rubbish. (rarely)
My sister rarely takes out the rubbish.

2 She empties the dishwasher. (always)
____

3 I vacuum the floor in my room. (often)
____

4 We clean the garage with Dad. (sometimes)
____

5 It's fun to look after our pets. (always)
____

6 We fold clean clothes. (often)
____

7 My brother is in the garden with Mum at the weekend. (sometimes)
____

> Häufigkeitsadverbien (*always, often, never, …*) stehen immer vor dem Verb.
> *Marcus often plays the guitar.*
> *I never eat meat.*
>
> **!** Ausnahme ist das Verb *be*. Hier steht das Häufigkeitsadverb dahinter.
> *I'm never late for school.*

► Check

Erklär-film

Challenge: Bedingungssätze Typ 1

Bedingungssätze (*conditional sentences*) bestehen immer aus zwei Teilen: einem Nebensatz mit *if* und einem Hauptsatz.

Bedingungssätze vom Typ 1 bildest du so:

If-Nebensatz: *simple present*	**Hauptsatz:** *will-future*
If you go to bed late,	*you'll be tired in the morning.*
If it rains tomorrow,	*my parents won't have a picnic.*

Mit Bedingungssätzen vom Typ 1 sagst du, was unter einer bestimmten Voraussetzung oder Bedingung passiert. Die Bedingung steht im Nebensatz. Im Hauptsatz steht die Folge aus der Bedingung.

▸ SB p. 171, p. 210

14 Challenge What will happen if ...?

Match the sentence halves. Write the right letters A–E into the boxes.
Ordne die Satzhälften zu. Schreibe die Buchstaben A–E in die richtigen Kästchen.

Der Hauptsatz kann auch vor dem *if*-Satz stehen. Das Komma fällt dann weg.
You'll miss your bus if you get up late.

1 If you want to get cheap clothes,
2 I'll sell my things
3 If we clean the floors now,
4 Mark will buy a new video game,
5 If she walks the neighbours' dog,

A she'll get some extra money.
B you'll have to go into a charity shop.
C if he gets some birthday money.
D we won't have to do it tomorrow.
E if I don't use them any longer.

1 ☐ 2 ☐ 3 ☐ 4 ☐ 5 ☐

15 Challenge At the charity shop

Read the conversation and circle the correct verb forms.
Lies die Unterhaltung und kreise die richtigen Verbformen ein.

Joana Look at all the cool video games in here, Mum! Can I buy one?

Mum If you buy / 'll buy a video game, do you have / will you have enough money for Dad's birthday present?

Joana I have £10. The games are £4.50. So I have / 'll have £5.50 for Dad's present if I get / 'll get a game. What should I do, Mum?

Mum If you aren't / won't be sure, maybe it is / will be best to check out how much the other things in here are.

Joana OK. If I find / 'll find something for Dad that isn't too expensive, I get / 'll get one of these video games too.

Five minutes later ...

Joana Dad wouldn't like anything in here, only the video games. But I have a fantastic idea! If I buy / 'll buy two video games, one for me and one for Dad, I have / 'll have a great present for him. And I play / 'll play two different games if I borrow / 'll borrow Dad's game!

▸ Check

16 REVISION Talking about jobs

Read the conversation. Complete the sentences with the correct will-future form of the verbs in brackets.
Lies die Unterhaltung. Vervollständige die Sätze mit dem will-future der Verben in Klammern.

Ms Bond This afternoon we (1)____________________ (talk) about jobs you'd like to do one day. Liam, what (2)____________________ (you / do) when you're older? (3)____________________ (you / be) a teacher like me?

Liam I love school, but I (4)____________________ (not work) in a school when I'm older. I think I (5)____________________ (get) a job as a nurse.

Ms Bond I'm sure you (6)____________________ (be) a brilliant nurse, Liam.

Liam Thank you.

Ms Bond Emma, what about you?

Emma I love art so I think I (7)____________________ (become) an artist. (8)____________________ (I / have to) go to university to be an artist?

Ms Bond No, some artists go to university and some don't. I think you (9)____________________ (love) university! But don't worry, you (10)____________________ (not need) to think about university until you're much older.

17 REVISION Jumbled sentences

Write sentences. Put the words and sentence parts in the right order. Use the will-future.
Schreibe Sätze. Bringe die Wörter in die richtige Reihenfolge. Verwende das will-future.

1 to our judo lesson / tomorrow / we / not go

____

2 you / at the football match / on Saturday / be / ?

____

3 you / do / next weekend / what / ?

____

4 Peter / his friends / at the youth club / this afternoon / meet

____

5 become / an architect / one day / maybe / I

____

6 at school / at 3 o'clock / wait / Mum and Dad / for us / ?

____

▸ Check

18 Revision What will you do?

Write five sentences about your future. What will or what won't you do when you have grown up? You can use the ideas in the box or your own ideas. *Schreibe fünf Sätze über deine Zukunft. Was wirst du tun oder nicht tun, wenn du erwachsen bist? Du kannst die Ideen aus dem Kasten verwenden oder deine eigenen Ideen.*

I think I'm sure Maybe	I'll I won't	live	in a big city / in a small village / in a different country / in New York / ...
		become	a nurse / a police officer / a famous musician / a firefighter / a mechanic / a gamer / ...
		have	a big family / a cool house / a dog / a fast car / ...

____

____

____

____

19 Revision Adverbs

Write adjectives or adverbs. *Schreibe Adjektive oder Adverbien.*

Adjective	Adverb
Be quick, we're late.	I'll walk (1) *quickly* ______, don't worry.
I'm (2) __________ !	I know, you're speaking nervously.
These are terrible news.	I'm (3) __________ sorry to hear.
Does she have a fast car?	Yes, she has. And she often drives it (4) ______ !
This picture isn't (5) __________ .	Can you see the picture clearly now?

20 Revision How did they speak or act?

Complete the sentences. Use the adverb form of the words in brackets.
Vervollständige die Sätze. Verwende die Adverbien der Wörter in Klammern.

1 'I love animals. I hope I'll be a vet one day!' said Noah __________ (excited) and he smiled.

2 'Lily sang __________ (beautiful) on the way to school,' said Ava.

3 'I want to play football. But where's my ball?' shouted Zane __________ (angry).

4 'I didn't do __________ (good) in the exams last week. I'll study harder next term,' said Lily.

5 'My bike isn't fast,' said Alice. 'Can we ride more __________ (slow), please?'

▶ Check

Hello again! The last day of the holidays

▸ Grammarmaster p. 4

Erklär-film

REVISION: Das present progressive

Mit dem *present progressive* sagst du, was jemand jetzt gerade tut. Du beschreibst damit auch, was auf Bildern passiert. Signalwörter für das *present progressive* sind: now (jetzt, gerade), at the moment (im Moment), today (heute).

Das *present progressive* besteht aus zwei Teilen:

be + verb + -ing

is watching

She's looking happy in the photo. (Sie sieht glücklich aus auf dem Foto.)

My parents aren't making lunch today. (Meine Eltern machen heute kein Mittagessen.)

What are you doing at the moment? (Was machst du gerade?)

be
I am / 'm not
he/she/it is / isn't
we/you/they are / aren't

▸ SB p. 11, p. 200

Unit 1 Travel and holidays

▸ Grammarmaster p. 5

Erklär-film

Das simple past mit *be*

Mit dem *simple past* sprichst du über Dinge, die in der Vergangenheit geschehen sind. Du verwendest es oft mit Zeitangaben wie yesterday (gestern), last week (letzte Woche), in 2022 (2022), ago (vor).

Das Verb *be* hat besondere *simple past*-Formen:

A **bejahte und verneinte Aussagesätze**

I / He / She / It / Noah / Mum	was / wasn't	at home.
You / We / They / My friends	were / weren't	at home.

B **Fragen**

	Was	he / she	at home?
	Were	you / they	at home?
Where	were	you	?

▸ SB p. 13, pp. 200–201

▸ Grammarmaster p. 6

Erklär-film

Das simple past: Bejahte Aussagesätze mit regelmäßigen Verben

Bei regelmäßigen Verben hängst du *-ed* an das Verb an. Es gibt nur eine Form für alle Personen:

I/you/he/she/it/we/you/they talked, looked, watched, ...

! Beachte:

- Endet das Verb auf *-e*, hängst du nur *-d* an: *smile → smiled, like → liked, save → saved*
- Bei manchen Verben wird er Konsonant am Ende verdoppelt: *plan → planned, stop → stopped, travel → travelled*
- Ein *-y* nach Konsonant wird zu *-ied*: *cry → cried, worry → worried, tidy → tidied*

▸ SB p. 14, p. 201

▸ Grammarmaster pp. 7–8

Das simple past: Bejahte Aussagesätze mit unregelmäßigen Verben

Einige Verben haben unregelmäßige Formen im *simple past*, z. B.:

do	→	did	forget	→	forgot
have	→	had	hear	→	heard
run	→	ran	read	→	read

Diese Formen musst du lernen.

▸ SB p. 14, p. 201, pp. 312–313

▸ Grammarmaster pp. 9–10

Erklärfilm

Das simple past: Verneinte Aussagesätze

Willst du sagen, dass etwas nicht geschah, stellst du didn't vor die Grundform des Verbs. *Didn't* verwendest du bei allen Personen.

Ben didn't like the food. (Ben mochte das Essen nicht.)

We didn't go out last Friday. (Wir sind letzten Freitag nicht ausgegangen.)

▸ SB p. 20, p. 201

Unit 2 Friends and heroes

▸ Grammarmaster pp. 12–13

Erklärfilm

Das simple past: Fragen und Kurzantworten

Fragen im *simple past* bildest du mit did und der Grundform des Verbs. Auf Entscheidungsfragen antwortest du mit Kurzantworten.

Did Gina visit her friends last week? – Yes, she did. / No, she didn't.
(Hat Gina letzte Woche ihre Freunde besucht? – Ja, hat sie. / Nein, hat sie nicht.)

▸ SB p. 52, p. 202

▸ Grammarmaster p. 14

Erklärfilm

Das simple past: Fragen mit Fragewort

Auch Fragen mit Fragewörtern bildest du mit *did*. Das Fragewort steht immer am Satzanfang.

Fragewort	*did*	Person	Verb im Infinitiv		
Where	*did*	*Lily*	*take*	*the photo?*	*(Wo hat Lily das Foto gemacht?)*
When	*did*	*she*	*take*	*the photo?*	*(Wann hat sie das Foto gemacht?)*

Wenn du nach dem Subjekt fragst (Wer oder was …?), dann bildest du die Frage ohne *did*.

Who helped Noah? (Wer half Noah?)

▸ SB p. 53, p. 202

▸ Grammarmaster p. 15

Erklärfilm

Indirekte Rede

Die indirekte Rede (*indirect speech*) verwendest du, wenn du berichtest, was jemand anderes sagt, schreibt oder denkt. Sätze in der indirekten Rede werden oft eingeleitet mit Verben wie *answer, say, tell sb., think*.

Melissa says (that) she likes her new school. (Melissa sagt, dass sie ihre neue Schule mag.)
The sign says (that) you can't sit here. (Auf dem Schild steht, dass man hier nicht sitzen darf.)

Personalpronomen, Pronomen und Verb musst du anpassen:

Peter says "I want to go to the library with my sister."
→ Peter says (that) he wants to go to the library with his sister.

▸ SB p. 51, p. 202

▶ Grammarmaster p. 16

Nebensätze mit Konjunktionen

Konjunktionen verwendest du, um Sätze miteinander zu verknüpfen. Die Wortstellung im Hauptsatz und im Nebensatz ist immer gleich: subject – verb – object.

subject	verb	object	Konjunktion	subject	verb	object
I	*have*	*a snack*	*when*	*I*	*'m*	*hungry.*
They	*got*	*the bus*	*because*	*they*	*didn't want*	*to walk.*
Simon	*practises*	*the guitar*	*so*	*he*	*can join*	*a band.*

▶ SB p. 57, p. 203

Unit 3 Activities and games

▶ Grammarmaster pp. 18–19

Das Futur mit going to: Bejahte und verneinte Aussagen

Erklärfilm

Das Futur mit *going to* besteht immer aus drei Teilen:

am / is / are am not / isn't / aren't	+ going to	+ Infinitiv des Verbs

Mit *going to* sagst du, dass du etwas in der Zukunft plangst (*after school, tomorrow, next week*).
I'm going to bedeutetet „Ich werde" oder „Ich habe vor".

I'm going to go to a holiday camp this summer. (Ich werde diesen Sommer in ein Ferienlager fahren.)
My parents are going to buy a new car next month. (Meine Eltern haben vor, nächsten Monat ein neues Auto zu kaufen.)
Holly isn't going to visit her grandma tomorrow. (Holly wird morgen ihre Großmutter nicht besuchen.)

▶ SB p. 82, p. 203

▶ Grammarmaster p. 20

Das Futur mit going to: Fragen und Kurzantworten

Erklärfilm

Bei Fragen stehen am, are oder is am Beginn des Fragesatzes, vor dem Subjekt.

Am I going to join the karate club? – Yes, I am. / No, I'm not. (Werde ich in den Karateclub eintreten?)
Is Peter going to meet Leo? – Yes, he is. / No, he isn't. (Hat Peter vor, Leo zu treffen?)
Are they going to make a cake for your party? – Yes, they are. / No, they aren't. (Haben sie vor, einen Kuchen für deine Party zu backen?)

▶ SB p. 83, p. 204

▶ Grammarmaster p. 21

Das Futur mit going to: Fragen mit Fragewort

Das Fragewort steht auch bei *going to* am Satzanfang.

What am I going to do? (Was werde ich tun?)
Who are you going to meet? (Wen wirst du treffen?)
Why is Zane going to talk to Ms Bond? (Warum wird Zane mit Frau Bond sprechen?)
Where are your teachers going to go? (Wo werden deine Lehrer hingehen?)

▶ SB p. 83, p. 204

▸ Grammarmaster pp. 22–23

Erklär-film

Die Steigerung von Adjektiven: Komparativ

Mit den Steigerungsformen der Adjektive kannst du Dinge oder Personen miteinander vergleichen.

A Bei einsilbigen Adjektiven und zweisilbigen Adjektiven, die auf *-y* enden, hängst du *-er* an. Beachte die Schreibweise:

old	*older (than)*	*My mum is older than my dad.*
easy	*easier (than)*	*I think English is easier than French.*
big	*bigger (than)*	*Emre's dog is bigger than Nila's dog.*

B Hat das Adjektiv drei oder mehr Silben oder zwei Silben und endet nicht auf *-y*, steigerst du es mit more.

famous	*more famous (than)*	*Spiderman is more famous than Captain Planet.*
expensive	*more expensive (than)*	*A car is more expensive than a bike.*
interesting	*more interesting (than)*	*This book is more interesting than the others.*

▸ SB p. 85, p. 205

▸ Grammarmaster pp. 24–25

Erklär-film

Die Steigerung von Adjektiven: Superlativ

Möchtest du sagen, dass etwas am besten, größten, teuersten usw. ist, verwendest du den Superlativ.

A Bei einsilbigen Adjektiven und zweisilbigen Adjektiven, die auf *-y* enden, hängst du *-est* an. Beachte wieder die Schreibweise:

old	*the oldest*	*Dima is the oldest boy in class.*
funny	*the funniest*	*Megastorm is the funniest superhero.*
big	*the biggest*	*We live in the biggest house in the road.*

B Hat das Adjektiv drei oder mehr Silben oder zwei Silben und endet nicht auf *-y*, bildest du den Superlativ mit most.

beautiful	*the most beautiful*	*Roses are the most beautiful flowers.*
important	*the most important*	*This is the most important competition of the year.*

▸ SB p. 86, p. 205

Unit 4 Celebrate!

▸ Grammarmaster pp. 28, 45

Erklär-film

Some / any

Wenn du über eine Menge oder Anzahl sprechen möchtest, du diese Menge oder Anzahl aber nicht genau kennst, verwendest du im Englischen *some* und *any*.

some
- bedeutet „einige", „etwas"
- in bejahten Sätzen
- wenn du um etwas bittest
- wenn du etwas anbietest

Zane invited some friends. (einige Freunde)
Can I have some biscuits, please? (einige Kekse)
Would you like some water? (etwas Wasser)

any
- bedeutet „kein", „keine", „keinen"
- in verneinten Sätzen
- in Fragen

My parents and I don't eat any meat. (kein Fleisch)
Are there any chairs in the classroom? (keine Stühle)

▸ SB p. 116, p. 206

▶ Grammarmaster p. 46

Erklärfilm

A little / a few

Du weißt schon, wie du über große Mengen sprechen kannst. Du verwendest dafür *much* für nicht zählbare Dinge und *many* für zählbare Dinge. Möchtest du aber über kleine Mengen sprechen, verwendest du a little und a few.

a little

- bedeutet „ein wenig", „etwas"
- bei nicht zählbaren Nomen, das heißt, du kannst von diesen Nomen keinen Plural bilden *(water, juice, music, love, money)*

I need a little fruit for my cake. (ein wenig Obst)
Can I have a little sugar for my tea, please? (etwas Zucker)

a few

- bedeutet „einige", „ein paar"
- bei zählbaren Nomen, das heißt, du kannst einen Plural bilden *(one apple, two apples)*

There were a few mistakes in your test. (einige Fehler)
There are only a few strawberries left. (ein paar Erdbeeren)

▶ SB p. 116, p. 206

▶ Grammarmaster p. 47

Zusammensetzungen mit *some* und *any*

Some verwendest du vor allem in bejahten Aussagesätzen, *any* findest du überwiegend in verneinten Aussagesätzen und in Fragen.

Dieselbe Regel gilt auch für Zusammensetzungen mit *some* und *any*.

- In bejahten Aussagesätzen: *somebody/someone, something, somewhere*
  There's somebody in the house. (Da ist jemand im Haus.)
  I can do something nice for my mum. (Ich kann etwas Schönes für meine Mutter machen.)
  My friend is somewhere in the classroom. (Mein Freund ist irgendwo im Klassenraum.)
- In verneinten Aussagesätzen und Fragen: *anybody/anyone, anything, anywhere*
  Is there anybody at school today? (Ist heute jemand in der Schule?)
  There isn't anything to eat! (Es gibt nichts zu essen.)
  Can you see my phone anywhere? (Kannst du irgendwo mein Telefon sehen?)

▶ SB p. 123, p. 208

▶ Grammarmaster pp. 48–50

Erklärfilm

Das present perfect: Bejahte und verneinte Aussagesätze

Mit dem *present perfect* sagst du, dass jemand irgendwann etwas getan hat oder dass irgendwann etwas geschehen ist. Der genaue Zeitpunkt des Geschehens ist unwichtig oder unbekannt.

Das *present perfect* besteht aus zwei Teilen:

I/you/we/they	have / haven't	+	3. Form des Verbs (Partizip Perfekt; Englisch: past participle)
he/she/it	has / hasn't		

Das past participle bildest du so:

- Bei regelmäßigen Verben hängst du -ed an den Infinitiv an, z. B.

play + ed → played	*We've played basketball a lot of times.*
visit + ed → visited	*Mara hasn't visited Brighton.*

- Bei unregelmäßigen Verben musst du die 3. Form lernen, z. B.

be → been	*Ahmet has been to Scotland very often.*
do → done	*I've done my homework.*
have → had	*My parents haven't had a car.*

▶ SB p. 119, p. 207, pp. 312–313

▶ Grammarmaster pp. 51–52

Erklärfilm

Das present perfect: Fragen und Kurzantworten

Entscheidungsfragen im *present perfect* beginnen mit *Have* oder *Has*.

Have you finished your homework? – Yes, I have. / No, I haven't.
Has Louisa met Paolo? – Yes, she has. / No, she hasn't.

▶ SB p. 121, p. 208

▶ Grammarmaster p. 53

Challenge: Das present perfect mit unbestimmten Zeitangaben

Das *present perfect* verwendest du mit unbestimmten Zeitangaben. Beachte die Stellung im Satz:

already	schon, bereits	*Dad has already bought flowers for Mum.*
just	gerade (eben), soeben	*I've just talked to him.*
not ... yet	noch nicht	*I haven't eaten yet.*

▶ SB p. 141

Unit 5 Getting ready for the future

▶ Grammarmaster pp. 56–57

Erklärfilm

Das will-future: Bejahte und verneinte Aussagesätze

Du verwendest das *will-future*, wenn du sagen willst, was in der Zukunft wahrscheinlich geschehen wird. Oft verwendest du es mit *I think, maybe, I'm sure.*

A **Bejahte Aussagesätze**

I / you / he / she / it / we / you / they	will / 'll	+ infinitive	*I think we'll stay at home tomorrow.* *It'll be rainy.*

B **Verneinte Aussagesätze**

I / you / he / she / it / we / you / they	will not / won't	+ infinitive	*I'm sure I won't become a programmer.*

▶ SB p. 148, p. 209

▶ Grammarmaster pp. 58–59

Erklärfilm

Das will-future: Fragen und Kurzantworten

Bei Fragen im *will-future* steht *will* am Satzanfang. Hat die Frage ein Fragewort, steht das noch davor.

	Will your sister be at the party? – Yes, she will.
	Will you meet Oscar tomorrow? – No, I won't.
When	*will she arrive? – At 8 o'clock.*
Where	*will we meet? – In front of the cinema.*

▶ SB p. 148, p. 209

▸ Grammarmaster p. 60

Adverbien der Art und Weise

Adverbien der Art und Weise beziehen sich auf ein Verb. Sie drücken aus, wie jemand etwas tut oder wie etwas geschieht:

She walked home slowly.
(Sie ging langsam nach Hause.)

"Oh, yes!" he said excitedly.
(„Oh ja!", sagte er aufgeregt.)

Die meisten Adverbien der Art und Weise bildest du, indem du -ly an das Adjektiv anhängst:

slow + ly → slowly

excited + ly → excitedly

!
- *-y + -ly → -ily: angry → angrily*
- *-le + -ly → -ly: horrible → horribly*
- Das Adverb zu *good* heißt *well*.
- Bei *fast* und *hard* haben Adjektiv und Adverb dieselbe Form.

▸ SB p. 155, p. 209

▸ Grammarmaster pp. 61–62

Die Wortstellung

Im englischen Aussagesatz ist die Wortstellung immer subject – verb – object: *I meet my friends.*

Eine Ortsangabe steht meist nach Verb und Objekt.

Subjekt	Verb	Objekt	Ort
I	*meet*	*my friends*	*at school.*

Zeitangaben stehen am Anfang oder am Ende des Satzes.

Zeit	Subjekt	Verb	Objekt	Zeit
Every day	*I*	*meet*	*my friends.*	
	I	*meet*	*my friends*	*every day.*

Stehen in einem Satz eine Orts- und eine Zeitangabe, kommt Ort vor Zeit.
Das ist wie im Alphabet: O kommt vor Z.

	Ort	Zeit
I meet my friends	*at school*	*every day.*

▸ SB p. 155, p. 210

▸ Grammarmaster p. 63

Erklär-film

Challenge: Bedingungssätze Typ 1

Bedingungssätze (*conditional sentences*) bestehen immer aus zwei Teilen: einem Nebensatz mit *if* und einem Hauptsatz.

Bedingungssätze vom Typ 1 bildest du so:

***If*-Nebensatz:** *simple present*	**Hauptsatz:** *will-future*
If you go to bed late,	*you'll be tired in the morning.*
If it rains tomorrow,	*my parents won't have a picnic.*

Mit Bedingungssätzen vom Typ 1 sagst du, was unter einer bestimmten Voraussetzung oder Bedingung passiert. Die Bedingung steht im Nebensatz. Im Hauptsatz steht die Folge aus der Bedingung.

▸ SB p. 171, p. 210